GØHRIL GABRIELSEN

TRANSLATED FROM THE
NORWEGIAN BY DEBORAH DAWKIN

Peirene

Ankomst

AUTHOR

Gøhril Gabrielsen was born in 1961, grew up in Finnmark, the northernmost county in Norway, and currently lives in Oslo. Her debut novel, *Unevnelige hendelser* (*Unspeakable Events*), won the Aschehoug First Book Award in 2006. Her second, *Svimlende muligheter, ingen frykt*, was published by Peirene Press in 2015 as *The Looking-Glass Sisters*. *Ankomst*, her latest novel and the winner of the 2017 Havmann Prize for the best book from the north of Norway, appears here for the first time in English. Gabrielsen's other awards include the 2010 Tanum Women Writers' Prize and the 2016 Amalie Skram Prize for her oeuvre as a whole.

TRANSLATOR

Deborah Dawkin trained as an actress and worked in theatre for ten years. She has written creatively and dramatized works. Her translation of Hanne Ørstavik's *The Blue Room* was published by Peirene Press in 2014 as part of the Coming of Age series. Other translations include *To Music* by Ketil Bjørnstad, co-translated with Erik Skuggevik, nominated for the Independent Foreign Fiction Prize 2010, and more recently *Story of a Marriage* by Geir Gulliksen and *The Bell in the Lake* by Lars Mytting. She and Erik Skuggevik have also co-translated eight plays by Henrik Ibsen for Penguin Classics. Deborah is currently working on a PhD on the translator Michael Meyer.

MEIKE ZIERVOGEL
PEIRENE PRESS

I love Gøhril Gabrielsen's writing. With deep psychological insight, she explores the darkest corners of her characters' psyche, illuminating them with her beautifully clear and precise language. And even though her stories are often about lonely places and people, Gøhril knows how to spin a good yarn, keeping the reader hooked until the last page.

First published in Great Britain in 2020 by
Peirene Press Ltd
17 Cheverton Road
London N19 3BB
www.peirenepress.com

ISBN 978-1-908670-58-8

Designed by Sacha Davison Lunt
Cover image: Vitalii Nesterchuk | 123RF.com
Typeset by Tetragon, London
Printed and bound by T J International, Padstow, Cornwall

This translation has been published with the financial support of NORLA

This book has been selected to receive financial assistance from English PEN's PEN
Translates programme, supported by Arts Council England. English PEN exists to
promote literature and our understanding of it, to uphold writers' freedoms around
the world, to campaign against the persecution and imprisonment of writers for
stating their views, and to promote the friendly cooperation of writers and the free
exchange of ideas. www.englishpen.org

GØHRIL GABRIELSEN

TRANSLATED FROM THE
NORWEGIAN BY DEBORAH DAWKIN

Peirene

Ankomst

1

This is where the world ends. From here there is nothing. An endless sea, edge to edge with cliffs and mountains, two extremes in a relentless conflict, in calm weather as much as in storm.

A light snowdrift fills the air, erasing the division between earth and sky. To avoid any risk of straying too near the edge, I park my snow scooter and trailer next to a boulder. It sticks up from the white-clad landscape, large and black. Hopefully it will be easy to spot even if the snow gets heavier.

The mountain slopes gently down towards the cliff edge. I strap on my snowshoes, adjust my headlamp and train its beam on each step I take into the greying twilight. The wind is against me. After a few metres I begin to miss the hum and shake of the scooter, conscious of the unpredictability of nature all around me.

I'm now standing five metres from the edge of the cliff, on an outcrop and next to a crevice that cuts into the mountain. A rock rises sheer and jagged out of the sea. I can make out the characteristic layers of shale, the slanting shelves and ledges that run side by side down into the water. I take a step closer to the edge and lean forward. Far below, the sea is crashing in with grey-black breakers. Ceaseless, ear-splitting breakers. When I put my hands over my sheepskin hat and press them to my ears, the booming sound comes through like a pulse pounding against my eardrums.

The rock seems empty, deserted, but I know that storm petrels overwinter there, hidden in the cracks and fissures. I know too that come May the din will be intense, the air filled with the shrieks of thousands of kittiwakes, cormorants, razorbills, auks and guillemots, and that I'll be here for months, measuring and recording the temperature, air pressure and wind speed, while I wait for the seabirds to return to their colony on land.

I look up and assess the cloud cover, the light fall of snow that pricks my nose and cheeks. Partly cloudy – or five eighths cloud cover. Which means there'll be good visibility in some areas and so a chance of getting a connection. I take the satellite phone from my inside pocket, hold it upright with its antenna turned to the sky and wait for a signal. After a couple of minutes I move, walk a few metres further on. I try again, holding the telephone vertically, searching, hunting. I go on like this, walking to and fro with my phone in the air, until two lines come up on the display. I take off my gloves and, standing as still as possible, write a message: *Have arrived. Track to bird colony cleared. Weather station and precipitation gauge will be up and working tomorrow. Everything OK. Big kiss.* I hit send, my thumb stiff in the freezing cold. The message disappears. I imagine the words – fragmented, morphed into indecipherable symbols and digits as they climb up between the snowflakes, slip through a gap in the clouds and on towards satellite heaven, to find their star, which in a flash scatters the message back to earth. Fully legible and comprehensible for Jo.

2

The reflective poles that I put out when I drove up the track shine like burning candles in the scooter's lights as I head down the mountainside. The return trip to the cabin goes without a hitch and only half an hour later I park outside. Down on the shore below, piled up on pallets, are my provisions: crates of food, gas, petrol and various pieces of equipment, brought here late last night by the captain, who lugged everything ashore and then, with a cursory nod, reboarded his boat to continue on his way. He's a man of few words, but our agreement was clear. He will return with fresh supplies every five weeks, his next visit being on 8 February.

As I watched the lights from his boat vanish into the darkness behind the headland, my isolation from the outside world became an unarguable reality. The nearest settlement is 100 kilometres away. In summer, on foot, the trip might take three or four days. In winter, especially during the darkest months, it would be plain irresponsible to venture out into this unmarked, impassable terrain. If, for some reason, I do want to leave, the sea will be my only option. But right now I'm not worried. The excitement of getting down to work, of having finally arrived, seventy degrees, fifty-eight minutes and thirty-six seconds north, far exceeds any possible misgivings about the distance between this peninsula and the sparsely inhabited fjords around me.

The sky in the south is shimmering with red and gold. The sun is on its return journey, so the evenings will slowly grow longer and the mornings lighter, until night merges with day in late April. An uplifting thought. I too shall expand, literally blossom, together with the surrounding nature. My footsteps glint in the snow from the shore up to the cabin. I follow them back down to the pallets, lift the plastic cover and run my hand over a couple of the crates. Small, choppy waves slip back and forth over the shallows, tugging at the kelp between the rocks and pebbles. A gentle rattling, that watery sound. I straighten up, feel the air fill my lungs, raw and icy cold. What am I waiting for? I should get going.

I've planned it precisely, the physical work. First, unpack my supplies and fill the trailer, then drive back and forth between the shed and the shore until the pallets are empty. Next stack the supplies and tools on the shelves, before unpacking the boxes of measuring instruments. As soon as everything's in place, I'll turn to my fixed day-to-day tasks: collecting firewood, maintaining the snow scooter, filling the generator with petrol, clearing the snow and generally keeping strict order, not least over the hours, the days and myself. The practical tasks must be portioned out, bit by bit. They act as an anchor in a daily existence

with no other obligations than to download meteorological data and carry out inspections of the weather station
and precipitation gauge. The seabirds will return to land
in three or four months. But before that, in just a couple
of weeks, there'll be two of us here.

The cabin and shed are surrounded by deep snowdrifts. I
had to dig my way to the front entrance last night, though it
wasn't deep enough to hold me back for long. A bluish tint
lies over the landscape now, and in the remaining twilight I
clear more space at the entrance and cut a path to the shed.
The shed is the only thing that remains from the few fami-
lies who lived here in the 18th and 19th centuries. In the
more recent past it's been regularly rented out to hunters
and fishermen – as I heard during my reconnaissance trip
here last spring. I take off a glove and run my fingers over
the outer wall. The panels have been splintered and worn
by the wind and weather. The shed door is fastened with
a rusty hook which comes loose easily enough, but I have
to put my shoulder to it before the door gives way with a
creak. I step in and turn up the power on my headlamp.
The cone-shaped light cuts sharply into the darkness,
revealing plain timber panelling, bare shelves that reach up
to the ceiling along one wall and a stack of firewood along
another. Further in, the beam of light falls on two stalls,
no doubt made for a couple of cows and some sheep. In
one corner I can see a grindstone, an axe and a pitchfork.
I let the light flit to and fro over the traces of daily lives
long gone – marks on the tools, the wear on the timber

stalls – and I confirm that the shed is nearly empty and suitable for my things.

The cabin, shaped like an L with a small outside toilet in the corner by the entrance, is built on the site of an old boathouse, with materials salvaged from houses that once stood here. It is solidly built, but very simple, and is showing signs of its age. The kitchen area consists of an old enamel sluice basin, rough-hewn cupboards under a countertop covered in old, cracked waxcloth, and opposite, beneath a long window, a relatively new portable gas cooker, next to a rickety side table with drawers. The seating area is larger but sparsely furnished. There is a long plank table, big enough for mealtimes and work. Two rocking chairs stand by the wood stove and two sets of shelves are fixed to the wall, with a rifle hanging between them. Next to the shelves is a window with a view of the fjord. A tiny alcove, separated from the living area by only a simple curtain, acts as a bedroom. A window with a view of the bay and lowland isthmus compensates for any lack of space. The landlord has followed the terms of our agreement precisely: the rooms are clean and tidy, the beds have new mattresses and the kitchen has had an upgrade, with two new saucepans, some glasses and cutlery.

Yesterday night, with just the light of a paraffin lamp and the feeble warmth from the stove, it was hard to imagine a practical working life here. But this morning, with the two electric wall lamps on and the generator humming in the background, I could picture us again as I had for so long: Jo and me, together, here in the cabin. Jo engrossed in writing one of his articles and me intent on my research. I imagine the way we might look up, the glances we might exchange, forgiving ourselves for the choices we've made.

The cloud layer thickens. The blue hour ebbs into an all-enveloping darkness and soon there's not a star to be seen. I put down my shovel and stamp the snow from my boots. It's half past one. My first working day is over. I go back into the cabin, sit in the rocking chair in front of the stove, blow on the embers and throw in a couple of logs. Out of habit, I take my phone from the shelf beside me and check the display. As expected, no connection. I put it back. Not that I'd have called him anyway. Electricity has to be rationed and communication by satellite is expensive. We made an agreement. After I've confirmed my arrival by text, we'll Skype at six o'clock on the third day, and thereafter we'll ring and Skype alternately, at the exact same time on dates with odd numbers – that is, if the cloud cover allows. This is my safety net. If he doesn't get an answer or I fail to contact him, it'll be down to difficult weather conditions or because something unforeseen has happened to me.

I fall asleep and wake up an hour later, confused and surrounded by darkness. Still not quite awake, in a kind of dreamlike state, I fix my gaze on the stove door and the light that flickers in the vent. I see myself from the outside, getting gradually smaller and smaller as I grow conscious of the huge distance between myself and everyone I have left behind.

3

6 January. A sharp, cold draught seeps in from the window over my bed. I automatically lift a corner of the curtain and peep out. There is, of course, not much to see. The sun is more than twelve degrees below the horizon. I lie still for an instant and feel the contrast between the cold of my nose and the warmth of my body under the duvet. Then, bracing myself, I throw off my bedclothes, swing my legs over the edge of the bed and put my feet straight down on the ice-cold floor. I sit there for a minute gazing up at the ceiling, until I have made a guess, said aloud to myself: Temperature minus three or four degrees, precipitation zero, a light wind from the south-east. I catch myself smiling as I dress, convinced that the thermometer and wind gauge will prove me right.

The bay lies wrapped in darkness, but in the light of the waxing moon I can make out the waves with frothy white crests rushing up into the shallows. They glide between the rocks on the shore and retreat with a pale metallic sheen. I attach the trailer to the scooter and load it up with the mast for the automatic weather station, along with my measuring equipment, guy wires and data logger, the bucket for the precipitation gauge, some antifreeze, my snowshoes, a couple of spades and a can of petrol. Before pulling on the protective cover, I check yet again that my equipment is properly secured. I don't want an abrupt turn or any sudden dips or humps to damage anything. I also make sure that the emergency beacon and some food and drink are easily accessible in the box under the scooter seat, and as a final precaution I run my hand over my inner pockets to check that my satellite phone, GPS and some extra batteries for the headlamp are where they should be. *Preparation and caution* is my mantra. I am now ready for what may be my most important trip to the bird cliff. I glance up at the sky. Cloud cover of six eighths, but no sign of snow clouds. Visibility good. I can drive and trust what I see.

Large parts of the trail have been erased by the incessant wind. I drive steadily, following the reflective poles, accelerating over snowdrifts. On the steeper slopes I have to stand up and rock the scooter to get a firm grip. When I finally arrive up on the plateau, the light beams from my scooter and my headlamp momentarily cross and then shoot off in different directions, confirming just how infinitely vast and desolate the landscape is out here. I turn my focus back on the reflector poles, and any hint of my tracks from the previous day. Eventually, I see the boulder. I stop and turn off the engine. Sweat is running down my spine. My face is stiff with the cold, but I can't resist. I unzip my scooter suit, take off my gloves and press my hands

against my cheeks, forehead and nose. For a few seconds I
feel the warmth of my palms burning against my skin, as
the icy wind blows through my woollen jumper and over
my stomach, shoulders, breasts.

The automatic precipitation gauge and anchor points for
the weather station were installed during the reconnaissance trip last spring. Now I have to find their location
using the GPS. They were set up with certain scientific
requirements in mind. Only time will tell if this is indeed
the optimal place from which to measure precipitation,
temperature, air pressure, humidity and wind speed. The
sea temperature – perhaps the most important variable – is
transmitted from a buoy via satellite to my PC.

The landmarks which I memorized on my trip in
spring – a slope and a high ridge – have disappeared in
the snowdrifts that now cover the landscape. I enter the
coordinates and, as I home in on the point displayed on
the GPS, I feel a tingle of joy at the concrete nature of the
task I have set myself, the hard facts that will now be my
focus. Diagrams, rising and falling columns, units, numbers, measurements in hectopascals, metres per second,
percentages and degrees Celsius. Clear and measurable
phenomena are what I want. The language of indisputable
realities, rather than dumb, undefinable feelings.

I walk a fair distance past the crevice that cuts into the
mountain and continue on beyond a wide ridge that
extends out towards the rugged cliffs. Here, at the highest

point, the wind takes hold and rushes towards me, making me gasp for breath. I move across the plateau, lifting my snowshoes, step by step, over the crusty snow in the direction of a south-facing slope. It's not far, but I have to stop several times and look around before the GPS tells me that I'm in the right place. For a second or two I feel utterly confused. There's nothing to focus on, everything is just snow and sky and sea. But as I bring a hand up to shield my eyes and stare into the whiteness, I spot the windscreen on the precipitation gauge, seemingly hovering over the wind-flattened slopes.

The horizon stretches out in an endless arc to the north. As the sea swells between the bird cliff and far-off continents, I dig out the weather station's anchor points, secure the mast and connect the sensors and battery before finally clearing away the snow that has settled on the precipitation gauge and installing the measuring bucket and antifreeze. It's a mammoth task, but eventually the two pieces of equipment stand fully operational and connected to the data logger, on a little patch pinpointed by a satellite but calculated by me. The image is powerful. Here we are. The elements and I. Together.

For years I have been waiting to complete my doctoral thesis. As an independent researcher, unaffiliated to any particular university or institution, I have had sole control over this project from day one. The freedom this gives me is enormous, but so too is the responsibility. I had to raise the necessary funding from various sources myself. But

I am convinced of the importance of this work; that my findings, when compared to data series collected twenty or thirty years back, will reveal connections that have never been documented adequately before. Findings that will contribute to our understanding of the impact of climatic changes on seabird populations and the effect of atmospheric conditions on their migration and nesting patterns. Kittiwakes, in particular, are now red-listed and considered an endangered species. The numbers of breeding birds have dropped by 80 to 90 per cent over a few decades and, as seabirds are indicators of the biodiversity of the ocean, this decline is extremely worrying. That is why I am here, near the bird cliff, at the northernmost tip of the mainland, in the middle of winter, alone. That is why I have cut loose, abandoned everything else for now, because the mapping of these meteorological parameters over a longer period will make a meaningful difference. I have told myself this so many times that I know it to be the truth.

Back outside the cabin, I sit on the scooter, open my inside pocket with numb fingers and check my satellite phone for the third time today. At last. An answer from Jo. But also a message from S. I open Jo's: *Glad you arrived OK. See you on Skype tomorrow. Hugs and kisses.* I read the text a few times before putting the phone back in my pocket. I can't face reading the other text yet. First I need to get inside and sort myself out. Make myself impenetrable. Strong.

I sit on the scooter for a while longer, listening to the waves, the rattle of the pebbles, the ceaseless wind, but also to the silence in the tightly packed snow all around me. I recall the sounds here last spring: the whispering of the grass in the breeze as it blew across the bay, the rustling in the brushwood as I followed the sound of a bluethroat near a rock. I managed to get right up close as it chirruped away, wagged its tail and then warned me with a sharp *tack, tack, tack*, followed by a soft *tweet, tweet, tweet*. When I was so close that I could have taken it, grasped it, the bird flew out of the bushes and flapped above my head, round and round. It hurts when I think about it. The courage of this solitary bird. Its nest and eggs were probably close by.

It's almost one o'clock. I go inside and unzip my scooter suit, letting it hang around my waist as I eat an orange at the kitchen counter. Then I pull my suit back on, go out, fix the headlamp over my sheepskin hat, strap on my snow-shoes and, using my poles, clamber over snowdrifts and sharp ridges of snow until I am on top of the mountain, some way behind the cabin. From here, in the purple-blue twilight and the sliver of moonlight, I can see the fjords stretching out along either side of the peninsula. A harsh, naked landscape – not a tree or bush in sight.

But as I stand here, I see hints of definition emerge: dips and depressions in the snow, the merest suggestion of shadows, vague angular outlines that mark the houses that once stood there. This scene gives me a sense of calm, of some kind of security, which is perhaps why I came up here. To prove that this place was once inhabited.

4

7 January. Anticipation of my Skype call with Jo this evening rises in perfect synchrony with my anxiety about the cloud coverage today. Several times I go to the front of the cabin and look at the sky for signs that the clouds might get heavier. But from where I'm standing the day seems promising. As does the weather forecast, although it doesn't cover this area, only the villages further in the fjords.

Observation, twelve o'clock: four eighths of the sky covered with wispy cirrus clouds.

Observation, two o'clock: two eighths covered by cirrus clouds.

Observation, five thirty: the faint rim of the waxing moon is barely visible through a thin layer of hazy cloud.

Between observations, I clear more snow, widening the path from the cabin to the shed, enlarging the parking space for the scooter. As my concern about the clouds and satellite connection lifts and the piles of snow around the cabin shrink, the forthcoming conversation magnifies in my mind. How will it go? What will I ask him and what might he answer? And, while I empty the last crates of equipment and arrange things on the shelves, how will he seem to me? How will he look as he listens and talks? Will he drag out his words, bring his hand to his face, look away, or be silent and still? I know myself only too well: I will scrutinize his every sentence, every facial expression, searching for what he really means, to see if he is holding something back. That's how it's always been. There's something in him that I can't figure out. A tension in him that causes the communication between us to vibrate.

Why would I expect him to be any different now?

Because it would be the *right* thing. He has to be more direct, show some grit, some sense of solidarity. After all, I've made the choice he is hesitating to make. Taken this trip away from my child, Lina. That must obligate him. Yes, I expect him to do the same. To leave his daughter, Maria, for these three or four months, to be together with me.

A quarter to six, by the table, I connect the satellite phone to my PC, search for a signal, hold the antenna straight up. A minute later one bar appears on the display. Hardly enough, I think, taking my equipment over to the kitchen area.

Here I repeat the procedure at the counter until two bars come up. I hesitate, still feeling uncertain. I look around and meet my own reflection in the mirror above the sluice basin. I run my fingers quickly through my hair, moisten two fingertips and smooth my eyebrows, then bite my lips until they are red and swollen. I wonder if he'll notice. My desire.

The screen emits a cold light into the darkened room. The contrast between the primitive and the civilized, the cabin and the technological world, is pronounced. As I call him, an intense joy rises up inside me. Joy for everything that lies behind us and for what is in store, the experiences that are to come, the time that we'll spend together out here.

His hair is dishevelled. He must have run his fingers through his fringe, several times, just before I called, something he often does when he's impatient or stressed. A sudden unease flexes in me, a steel wire winding itself round my solar plexus. But as he smiles and his eyes light up the way they do, I catch myself smiling back in the corner of the screen, and when he leans forward and says that the fresh air has done me good, I feel the wire slacken. Reassured and happy, I start to talk about my first trips to the bird cliff. I describe the wind, its raw energy, and the counterforce with which I meet each gust. I describe the light, as delicate as the glimmer in mother-of-pearl, and how the snow-covered expanse and the sky merge into infinite space beyond the plateau. The divide is barely visible, I say, watching myself stretch out my hands and curl my fingers, as though to grasp this feeling of infinity. Just wait, I continue without pause, you'll love it, this whole place.

I straighten up, take a breath. He looks back at me expectantly, then stares at me for several seconds, cold and distant, until I realize that the screen has frozen. I tell him. There's a disturbance on the line, I say, you've frozen, and push on with the conversation towards the immobile expression on the screen, but in a voice that seems suddenly harsh and strained.

Me: And Maria, how's she doing?

Jo: She's good. We've been on several skiing trips.

Me: Oh, that's great.

Jo: Yes, she's really keen. She did two kilometres yesterday.

Me: So will you have her more often now? Before you leave?

Is the picture still frozen or is he back? Is it just a trick of the light, that vague flicker I see in his eyes?

Me: You still haven't come to a clear agreement with Gry?

Jo: I can't leave until I know my daughter is OK – that's just how it is.

My daughter... He says it with such intensity, such certainty. As though his love for Maria is greater, more serious, than mine for Lina. Or that my ability to care is weaker, of a lower quality, than his. Maybe what he wants to say is that separation from our children isn't to be taken lightly. Or is it my own conscience that's niggling me? A sense of guilt that I can't, won't, relate to?

Jo: Hey, you. Are we going to end like this?

The picture jumps, his face starts to move jerkily. I catch myself studying the fullness of his lower lip, the crooked teeth that come into view, until the image freezes again and he stares blankly at me with half-closed eyes.

Me: No, I'm sorry. I'm just so looking forward to you coming.

When our call is over I don't turn off the PC, despite the drain on the power supply. I leave the screen open and luminous as I go into my alcove and lie down. I don't want to break the contact, imagining that the signals continue to hover like an invisible link between the cabin, the sky and his house. But when I close my eyes, it's the image of Lina I reach for. The delicate, fine hair that tangles so easily, the smile, the soft cheeks and sticky-out ears, the look of amazement on her little face when I come to pick her up from S's. Then, as sleep sneaks in and consciousness slips away, it's Jo that I see.

5

8 January. Among the maps and paperbacks on the shelf here, I have found a local history pamphlet and at breakfast, as I drink my coffee, I pick it up and leaf absentmindedly through its pages. An article about the bird cliff catches my eye. With interest, I read the descriptions of the people who settled out here in the 18th and 19th centuries, their hardships and day-to-day lives. The last paragraph tells the story of a fire in the winter of 1870, which destroyed the home of settlers Olaf and Borghild Berthelsen, their five daughters and little son, Niels. The fire was fatal, culminating in another tragedy the following year. The sparse text does not reveal how or why.

I push my plate aside and pull the pamphlet closer. I reread this dramatic piece several times and, when I have finished, the image is so strong that I can see it right there in the window, in the reflection of the light from the wall lamps. The incident that took place long ago, across the way; the small cluster of people who gathered in the snow under a black night sky. Borghild Berthelsen, who counted her children, one by one, in the glowing red heat of the devouring flames.

I put the pamphlet down, rise from the table and go over to the kitchen counter. I pour some melted snow into the pan, light the gas and boil up the water for my first batch of washing-up since my arrival: two glasses, one cup, some cutlery and a couple of plates, which I rinse in a large saucepan and put out to drain on a tea towel. With my hands in the scalding-hot water, my skin going wrinkly, I think of how hard it was back then, especially during the winter. Washing nappies, cooking, endless housework, looking after children and farm animals. Chapped fingers against rough fabrics, splintered wood and coarse surfaces, the relentless switch between extreme heat and cold. A ceaseless struggle in infinite darkness at the furthest edge of the world.

I go over to the basin. I pour in more meltwater and wash my face, brush my teeth and gather my hair into a ponytail, before finally getting dressed. As I pull my woollen jumper over my head and catch my reflection in the mirror, I try to imagine her, Borghild Berthelsen, who lived here more than 140 years ago. She was probably my age, but already exhausted and ground down after giving birth to so many children, six in all. I imagine her face was taut, her skin pale and transparent, her hands thin, her nails tinged with blue and rimmed with black. Or was she largely unmarked by all the births and struggles? Was she small and energetic, tough and strong, like me? After putting on my jacket, gloves and hat, I continue to see her in my own movements: the way she opens the door one January morning, goes out, breathes in the smell of the sea, feels the cold air prick and bite her cheeks. I see her striding across the snow in a coarse, heavy woollen skirt with a shawl wrapped around her shoulders, going into the shed and re-emerging with an armful of logs, returning to the cabin and putting them in a basket by the stove. Just as I do. When I open the stove door and put in a couple of logs, I think how she too sat like this, on her knees, as she blew the embers to kindle a flame.

With a sudden burst, the fire is vibrating in the burner. I get up and look around, knocked off balance by these vivid, almost tangible images. I can't go on like this. If I'm to survive the isolation until Jo gets here, I can't seek the company of people long gone.

6

Meteorology. The science that uses physical and mathematical models to forecast the weather and interpret atmospheric phenomena: cloud patterns, storms, polar lows. I stand at the long window in the kitchen, contemplating the snowy wind that tears thick and white across the bay outside. Tracing with a finger the rime on the glass pane, I say aloud, in a voice hoarse from underuse: Emotions should be like that too. Measurable. Predictable.

I pace back and forth between rooms, open cupboard doors and drawers, browse through the books again, the magazines on the shelf, before stopping in front of the rifle. I take it down from the wall, place the butt against my shoulder and with my index finger on the trigger, I position myself opposite the window and take aim at my own reflection. I lower it with a shiver, run my hand over the barrel and chamber and conclude that it's rust-free. A little-used hunting weapon, no doubt. I scan the cabin again, this time for ammunition. I find three cartons at the back of a kitchen cupboard, sixty cartridges in total, and decide to practise shooting one day when the weather is clear and mild. I might enjoy it. I have a hunting certificate and for a while I was a member of a team with S.

I sit down at the plank table and stare into the room. I feel a growing sense of restlessness and start to tap my fingers hard against the wooden surface. Something about the situation, my agitated movements, drags my thoughts back involuntarily to my birthday about a year ago, when I told S that I wanted a divorce. We were sitting opposite each other at the dining table, with Lina in her highchair between us. I was sitting just as I am now, restless, distracted, with a fork in my hand. I poked it into a slice of chocolate cake again and again, until my plate was covered with crumbs. I hadn't planned to say it so directly. But there was something about the situation, the way the evening had unfolded. What had been done and not done, said and not said, the atmosphere between us in the cramped living room. So, as Lina, almost two years old, was busy turning a page of her picture book, I said: I don't want to go on any more. I want a divorce.

The cake swelled on the table, dark-brown icing sweating in the heat of the tea lights. S had made it the night before from a packet; all he had added was melted butter and a splash of water. There was something about that. The demonstrative pride with which he placed it before me. My show of pleasure was like the icing, smeared on, smooth and fake, covering a dried-out, crumbly interior.

I lifted Lina out of her highchair, put her on my lap to shield her from what I was about to do. But she laughed as I said: I'm in love with someone else.

I get up from the table and look out of the window. The wind is still raging out there. The trail to the bird cliff is snowed in again and the reflector poles will be hard to spot amid the swirling snow. I could stay here, safe in the cabin, but the data needs to be collected and regular inspections are paramount as snow and ice can cover the precipitation bucket and envelop the temperature and humidity meters, the wind gauge can freeze up, and even a light breeze of thirteen metres per second can damage the sensors. I check the barometer. Low pressure. The wind isn't about to let up any time soon. There's nothing to do but wait.

As if to confirm this thought, I hear a piece of roofing felt come loose in the wind. It slams into the gable again and again, before it stops suddenly and falls silent. Not like S, who never gave up. He slammed the table, the doors and walls, hard, with a clenched fist, for weeks afterwards, even when I told him clearly that I wasn't going to be moved, that there was no way back. Lina was usually there. She'd tremble, stick her fingers in her mouth and stare at us with large, anxious eyes. I too could slam tables, as I yelled that he couldn't expect any consideration when he gave none himself. Our home turned into a bad-weather zone. We were two equally matched storm centres, each revolving in our own half of the house, raging, wreaking havoc, until we met midway and, after a violent clash, spun off in opposite directions. A kind of Coriolis effect, in which ocean and air currents in the northern hemisphere twist to the right and those in the southern hemisphere to the left.

For example:

I went into the bedroom and locked the door. He came after me, stood outside breathing heavily, pulled on the handle, kicked the door frame, demanded I open up and let him in. Eventually, to calm him down, not least for Lina's sake, I opened the door. He burst in, grabbed me and threw me onto the bed. He pinned me down with his full weight and an arm across my chest, while with his free hand he tore at my clothes. I gasped for breath, twisted and writhed, and with a strength that came from deep inside, I managed to extricate my right arm and drive my elbow into his neck. He crumpled and, whimpering like a wounded animal, rolled over to one side of the bed, while I went to the other. For a few seconds we lay there panting before, wordlessly, we each retreated to our own part of the house.

7

I'm sitting at the window with my feet up on the table and a cup of coffee in my lap, half dressed in my thermal underwear. I still haven't switched on the ceiling or wall lights. I don't need them. During the last few days my eyes have adapted to the faint difference between the surrounding darkness outside and the sparse light indoors.

Besides, my thoughts seem clearer, more focused and visual, when I'm unplugged from the civilized world. Electricity, my PC and satellite phone are a disturbance.

I can't stop thinking about her and him, Borghild and Olaf. It was here in the bay, within those barely visible depressions in the snow, that it all took place. One hundred and forty years is a long time, but the story in the pamphlet, and the few short lines that describe the start of their life together, trigger a stream of images: *Soon after they were married, he went out to the fishing bay where they planned to settle, and built a house and shed, and cleared grazing land for a horse and some cows and sheep.*

Borghild arrived a couple of months after him, following a long and arduous journey, first by steamboat, then by horse and cart and finally by a *jekt* over the fjord. She was probably no more than nineteen or twenty and would never have travelled so far from home. She was raised in a little town, perhaps, with streets and horse-drawn carriages, and shops where fine woollen weaves and dress fabrics could be bought, as well as sugar, salt herrings and potatoes. Not like this place, a far-flung corner of the country where she had to learn to spin and weave and work the barren soil, and where the boat trip to the nearest trading post took several hours.

I see it all from a bird's-eye view, the journey along the coast, Borghild standing at the railing of the boat, her gaze turned towards land. The prow cutting through the water, churning up waves that spread like the wings of a gull, swooping over the sea's surface. And I see him, Olaf, the nest builder, many miles away. The man who has spent the whole spring building their house, thinking of her as he laid one log upon another, the children they will have, the joy and warmth that will fill the rooms that he has insulated with the finest moss. Later that summer, when the house and shed are finished, he stands in the tall grasses and sees the *jekt* with its white sails heading down the fjord. He casts a quick glance over the windowsills, stairs and banisters to check that they are solid enough, good enough, before he runs his hands through his hair, tightens his shirt collar and the cord in his trousers. The *jekt* glides into the bay and he wades barefoot into the icy shallows, his shirtsleeves wet as he reaches a hand out to the woman who stands at the railing and waits. He carries her all the way to the shore, her laced boots bobbing up and down beneath the hem of her skirt, which is lifted by the wind as she sets foot for the first time on the verdigris grass. She straightens her waistband and smiles shyly at the man who offers her his arm as they walk together to the house, up the front steps, through the door and into rooms smelling of fresh pine with droplets of resin still seeping from the log walls. And, while the seabirds fly back and forth to the bird cliff and the night sky drifts over the grass roof, shifting from midwinter darkness to a pale midnight sun, they lie beneath sheepskins in fierce embrace, over and over. His hand on her belly, life stirring within. And the trundle beds are constantly widened as more children arrive to fill them. And in the background the waves come roaring in, steadily, like a clock, minute by minute, hour by hour, right up until today, this moment in which I see it all from the same place.

Now I see Jo before me. Jo on our first meeting. A meeting so ordinary, so everyday, that I could easily have overlooked him. I noticed him in a queue for the kiosk at the arts centre in the interval of a children's play. I had seen him a couple of times before, in the canteen at a research institute I used to attend. Now here he was, clearly with his own daughter, standing in front of Lina and myself. It was Maria's enthusiasm that struck me first, the way she slipped in and out of her father's grasp, making him spin her round, doing cartwheels right there in the queue. And then Jo himself, with his unique attentiveness, on which I am now so hooked. He was without doubt totally and utterly focused on Maria. Patient and devoted, and yet I sensed a certain restraint in him. There was something in his movements, something distant, removed, which seemed confirmed by his gaze as he turned to apologize for bumping into us.

I recognized him the instant I saw him again a few months later. I was with Lina, walking round a lake on the outskirts of town, and I glimpsed him sitting on a bench by the path. He was holding a bag of bread and Maria was running back and forth, grabbing handfuls of crumbs to scatter before the ducks. I didn't react at first, not consciously at least, apart from registering a pressure in my chest. Then I became aware of the sound of the pushchair's wheels on the gravel gradually going quiet. It was only when I had come to a complete halt that I realized I was staring. At him. I saw it even more clearly now. The sensitivity, the devotion, but also something closed, something that was turned towards another place entirely. This contradiction in him, this duality – presence and absence, devotion and distance – appealed to me so strongly that all I knew was that I too wanted to be seen like that. I wanted to be that other place.

I sat down on a bench nearby, parked the pushchair, did not hide away or go home, but planted myself as close as I could, facing him and Maria and the continuing game. I shivered in the cold wind and pulled my scarf about me. He turned, smiled, said something about the early autumn. I rubbed my fingers, stared up, looked around. And then it leaped out at me, in red and orange and yellow, leaves that fell, leaves that floated, fragile and brittle leaves, their veins like febrile nerves, leaves high in the treetops that spread towards the open sky, that reached towards the last sparkle of sunlight on gnarled and trembling branches. Everything was saying: Hurry! Hurry!

There's a mouse in the kitchen cupboard, I've heard it several times while sitting at the table. The sounds of rummaging among the washing-up brushes and in the box of candles. Those sharp little claws on the woodwork, that mouth, those tiny teeth sinking into tallow, gnawing on bristles, ripping them apart. It is doubtless a distant relative of the mice that once lived in the house that Olaf built out here in the bay. One of an almost endless cycle of litters of pink baby mice. Or were they all burned and turned to ashes along with the rest of the house? I get up from my chair and slam the cupboard door in an attempt to scare it away.

8

10 January. Eleven o'clock. Observation at the cabin. Temperature: minus eight point eight degrees Celsius. Wind: a moderate breeze from the north-east, about six metres per second. Cloud cover: zero.

I am outside the front door, fully dressed and with my photographic equipment and PC in a rucksack on my back. On the fjord the frost-mist drifts like fine candy-floss and above me the full moon is silvery in an ice-blue, star-filled sky. A feathery layer of rime has formed on the outside walls and my footsteps over to the scooter are accompanied by the squeak of rubber soles against dry, frozen snow. I stop. The air pricks and tears at my throat like a thousand tiny drills, then streams out of my mouth in little white clouds. I feel the moisture freezing around my nose, a sensation that is amplified by a sharp, biting wind. I remove my gloves, take a balaclava from a pocket and pull it over my head, before putting my fur hat back on and tying it firmly under my chin.

I settle myself on the scooter and press the start button. It immediately jerks into action. Exhaust fumes swirl thick and red around my rear lights. Slowly I drive past the cabin, glance towards the window of the living area and shudder when I catch sight of my reflection in among the frost roses. Masked. Disguised. As though on my way to commit a crime. Perhaps I am already a criminal, the crime already committed. Guilty of an unlawful act, I must flee, run away. I feel my fingertips on the steering bar, stiff and uncooperative in the cold. The reflection is right. All is not as it seems. Despite my conviction that I am here for a specific task, I am also driven by other, very different motives. Motives as hidden as the life in the depths of the expanse of ocean visible in the distance.

As the scooter becomes more biddable under me, lighter and faster, I come up to a half-standing position and push the skis through deep snowdrifts, over hardened slopes. The effort, the tightness of my thighs, the up and down motion. I see myself sitting astride Jo, pushing my crotch against him until his cock is rigid and hard deep inside me. I rock back and forth, his hands in mine, his face under mine. I possess him, own him. For one long moment he is helpless, wholly devoted to my body and to me. I have waited for a year and six months to have free access to him. To have some hours or days alone, just the two of us, without interference from Gry or S, without Maria and without Lina. As my front lights tear into the twilight, I accelerate, pressing the scooter up the final steep slope. When I reach the top of the plateau and look back, the horizon glows blood-red towards me.

*

I park near the boulder, take out my GPS and enter the coordinates, then turn north towards the indicated position. Jo and I are from the same town, south of here. He lives in a terraced house on the west side, I rent a two-room apartment in the east. He kept the house after his divorce from Gry four years ago. She lives just a stone's throw away, and since Maria is free to come and go between these two homes, he has no intention of moving. I have moved as far as I can from S. Six months after filing for divorce, I let him buy the house we owned at market value. Let him keep most of the furniture, almost all our possessions, the material things: kitchen equipment, pictures, books. I had no choice. Not when I'd left him for another man. If I wanted to be free, I had to buy myself out of my betrayal and the family we had once wanted to be. That, at least, is the obvious explanation. But more than anything else, I let him have what he wanted because of a series of specific events. Episodes without particular cause, without conflict or our usual face-offs. Episodes that, like a sudden inexplicable shadow, left me with the desire to get away as fast as possible.

For example:

One evening, just before I moved out, we were on our way home from the summer end-of-term party at Lina's nursery when he suddenly turned off the main road, onto a narrow dirt track towards the fjord. Sitting in the back seat, all I could see in the rear-view mirror were his eyes, eyebrows tightly knitted, gaze fixed beyond the road and our surroundings. He was driving fast. The bushes scraped against the car doors and we lurched forward, bouncing up and down in our seats over the bumps. Nothing was said. Even Lina went quiet in the front. But a couple of kilometres on, I plucked up the courage. My voice filled the whole car – I was surprised that it sounded so soft and intimate. Where are we going? I heard it ask. I don't know, he answered, sounding almost surprised. But then, as though I'd reminded him of something, something he'd forgotten, he stopped and turned off the engine. He sat rigid, staring straight ahead, while his fingers searched for the door, fumbled with the handle. With a sharp click, the child lock was on and he was outside looking in. He went round the bonnet, along the length of car and, more decisive now, stopped at my window, took the handle and held it, standing with his suit jacket pressed to the glass, ready to tear open the door. I fixed my gaze on Lina, her skin, so pale, so delicate and soft. It was almost unbearable. I looked away, dry-eyed, towards the rocks, the bushes outside the window, and then further out, towards the sky and the end of the road, as though seeking some kind of help from them. But they stared back, unwilling witnesses to whatever was about to happen. I mustered my defences, a breastplate for protection. I wasn't about to surrender without a fight. But then it didn't happen, the thing I feared. Instead, S was suddenly back in the driver's seat. S and his body, rigid at the wheel. S and his voice, mumbling to itself: I must pull myself together. I must pull myself together now. S and his hands that turned the key in the ignition, lifted the handbrake, went into reverse and drove quietly back to the main road.

I spot the top of the weather station and then the windscreen on the precipitation gauge, poking out from the snow dunes that have built up around the masts. Drawing closer, I see the sparkle of crystallized ice on the metal and hoarfrost like tiny, sharp saw blades on the sensors and guy wires. Carefully I loosen the shards, brush them away, and they fall onto the packed snow with a tinkling sound, like the chiming of little bells.

I set about my tasks. I check that the precipitation bucket is level and tipping smoothly, that the antifreeze is free of snow and slush, then connect the PC to the data logger and transfer the latest measurements. Finally, I pull the camera out of my rucksack, take off the lens cover, switch on the flash and slowly, turning 360 degrees from north to east, from south to west, I capture the landscape. The snowdrifts, the plateau, the edge of the mountain. The gradual re-emergence of the rock face, the transition from white upon white to the first patches of spring brown, must also be documented, week by week, and presented alongside my numerical data.

I put the camera and PC back in my rucksack, fingers devoid of all sensation, almost blue from the cold and the sharp, creeping wind. I put them against my lips and for a moment breathe warmth into my palms. Yes, I am here to understand the workings of the outer, physical world.

But there is also a deep pain and purpose that outstrips any practical motive. A motive that involves an escape and a separation from Lina and a desire as blood-red as the sky above me.

9

I wake up one morning with the feeling that someone is standing by my bed, tugging at the duvet. Still half in a dream, I instinctively lift the duvet a fraction to make space for something, and a child creeps in beside me, small and soft, followed by a cold draught. Frozen, as if in a membrane of ice, I open my eyes and stare at the ceiling and out into the room, into the present, until I feel the icy film crack and slip off me in tiny jangling pieces.

A dream. I sit on the edge of my bed, grab the water glass from the shelf next to it and take a few sips, allowing the liquid to roll around my mouth as I squint at the clock. Six. I might as well get up. Perhaps listen to the news on the radio. Drag real life into the cabin. It's time now. I've been buzzing with daydreams and memories. I need factual observations. The temperature. Wind speed. Cloud cover. They steady the world. Like the water that now glides cold down my throat, filling my stomach.

A dream. Or something dreamlike. The dawning day, the light that rises on the horizon, transparent and sheer with a hint of pale blue. Like the light that surrounds a newborn baby. Like the light I see Lina in. These are my thoughts as I stand there at the kitchen counter. But do these thoughts occur to me at the same time as I look down and see a strand of hair in the butter on my knife, or a nanosecond before? The hair is thin and fine, almost invisible. I go over to the lamp above the cooker and hold the knife to the light, turn my wrist, examine every millimetre of the blade. With two fingers in a pincer grip, I slowly pull the hair out of the sticky mass. Roll it between my fingers and feel its texture. It is identical to the one I found on my keyboard the previous day. It was just lying there, diagonally across the letters B, H, U, like some sort of greeting. A child's hair, but darker than Lina's. Yesterday I threw it in the stove. And I do the same again now. I open the stove door. Watch the strand of hair curl up and turn to ashes on the embers.

It strikes me. Occurs to me. That coincidence is a variable I ought to be aware of from now on.

10

During the long hours when I'm not working, writing or reading, I drift into thoughts of Olaf and Borghild, the family that once lived out here. I catch myself at it quite regularly, despite the effort I make to push such thoughts away. Perhaps the images are so vivid because of my proximity to the location. I am utterly gripped by the descriptions in the old pamphlet. There is something in them that touches me beyond the words. The fantasies they inspire are unusually compelling and seductively unfamiliar.

I'm sitting in front of the stove when it starts again. Tired, a little drowsy, with my head leaning against the back of my chair, I see images flicker past, clear and intense. Not in full colour or even black and white, but in soft hues which I can decide myself. The shirt might be pale blue. The shawl red. The voices, by contrast, are loud and assertive. All around me is an orchestra of background sounds: the crackling of a log fire, the whinnying of horses, the bleating of sheep, sawing and hammering, children playing in the endless roar of the waves. And as I sink into my chair in the comfort of the glowing stove, warmth streaming through my clothes and over my face and hands, I can feel it in every fibre of my body: the sun that washes over the bay, a deluge of light on the two of them as they sit against the south wall of their house on a mild summer's day. The ever-present wind glides icily past. They shudder, perhaps from joy as much as from the cold, because out there in the bristling grass, soon to be mowed and dried in the sun, their five daughters are scampering about, while their first son, their baby boy, lies sleeping indoors.

Her bosom heaves sweetly beneath her dress, his arms are rough and strong. The bare skin, her ankles, his neck. Does he take her hand in his, give her fingers a gentle squeeze, a secret signal? They get up, amble towards the shed, smile shyly, open the door and sneak in. She leans against the beams of the stall, her back arched, breasts like two buoys where he can drop anchor. He steps forward, breathes in the hollow of her neck, presses closer, hard, stiff, and there, right there, he pulls up her skirts with one hand, while the other glides between her thighs and parts her gently with two light fingers as he slowly enters her. Her desire swells, the floor sways, she moans and gasps, the contours of their faces flicker, slip away. It is not two strangers I see, but Jo and myself.

I sink further into my chair, close my eyes. Jo, I whisper, and run my hands over my midriff, over my belly. But the image is scrambled. He has withdrawn and now he leaves me, abandons me there in the shed. My fantasy suddenly seems thin and fragile, betrayed by the cold reality of lived experience. I can't hold him back, no matter how hard I try. He goes out into the sunshine, walks over the slopes, onto the grass, laughs and stretches his arms out to the child who comes running towards him. Maria.

It is hot by the stove. I wriggle out of my jumper, roll up my sleeves and sink back into my chair. I want to see Jo, to conjure him up, but his image fades like thin lines on rough, ribbed paper. When I try again, when I concentrate, it's not Jo I see but S. He walks towards me, with Lina sitting on his shoulders, as she so often does, back rounded, with tangled hair like a halo round her head, chubby hands firmly around her father's neck, her cheek against his head, as he talks and points, this way and that. I hear their voices, one a deep bass forced into a higher register, the other with a bright and bell-like tone. I see myself trotting at their side, stretching up to her, also pointing and talking, in a voice I cannot hear but which I watch rising and falling in hertz and decibels on an audiogram. As we walk further, I babble about things Lina can neither grasp nor understand, phrases and words from scientific articles, statistics and theories. I talk and talk, and S's and Lina's voices are silenced. Soon they are gone, leaving me bent over my work at the plank table, behind my PC and stacks of books, reaching out to something else, to phenomena, events, to the bird cliff.

11

Things may be known, but not yet acknowledged. My research has its roots in this very observation. A creature may be rare and unique, and yet still be perceived as an unremarkable feature in its habitat, just another part of the local biodiversity. This same creature only becomes what it is, rare and unique, when someone consciously classifies it as such.

In the active phase of my research, during data collection, before I become embroiled in analysis and conclusions, I often find myself giving my research aims dizzying dimensions. I want to understand life itself, its physicality, its biology, things that the continuous flow of impressions and sensations can never truly explain. I want to define it in relation to time and place, and then to make it concrete by repeating my measurements, weighing it, arriving at a conclusion that is 100 per cent accurate. I relate to life as though I were in a dream and then I attempt, by all means available, to wake up and understand what makes the dream possible. I want to investigate, identify, reveal and gain a clarity through my findings. Not only do I want my work to be perceived as an important turning point, but I want it to give my own life a new and unexpected direction.

If this were to happen, I might do something completely different. Abandon any seemingly objective, static research to roam around remote lands, to ride this way and that across the steppes and tundra, feeling the horse's rocking motion over green grasslands as I breathe in the dry inland air with the smell of manure and earth, and then in the evening to kneel in a nomad's tent, clad in a garment decorated with embroidery and braids, with a cup of sheep's milk in my hands, listening to the fitful guttural speech of the women, which, in some purely external and unscientific way, might confirm that I, the stranger, was included among the unique.

12

Seabirds are affected by climate on different levels in time and space. Large-scale changes are often due to variations in atmospheric circulation, which in turn affect sea temperatures and currents over larger regions. The North Atlantic Oscillation is an important factor in the weather throughout the North Atlantic, and it has been documented that the survival of a number of species of seabird in the northern sea varies in correlation with the NAO winter index.

A collaborative project between meteorologists and ecologists has, however, offered new insights into the climate's impact on seabirds.

A traditional method in climate research is to take identical measurements of weather conditions at a number of geographical points, creating point maps. The new method takes the results from these point maps and compares them with changes in animal populations. For this project, the researchers focused on a data series on guillemots, a critically endangered seabird whose population has declined by 90 per cent since the 1960s. In the winter of 1986–7 a large number of starved guillemots were found dead in the sea. Scientists looking at the data for links between this event and changes in the climate found that there had been a unique weather phenomenon in the Barents Sea that winter: an increased incidence of high pressure in the area and simultaneously many polar low pressures. On closer examination, a clear connection was found between this weather phenomenon and the mass death of guillemots. This confirmed that traditional research methods *combined* with the NAO index offered a better understanding of how changes in climate might affect seabirds. This is the approach that I intend to utilize – an approach that requires me to be a meteorologist as well as a biologist, my first discipline.

13

I am waiting all the time. Waiting for the sun and for brighter days. Waiting for the wind to abate and the snow to stop. Waiting for data and measurements, for dates with odd numbers, for satellite calls, Skype calls, the voice and the face of Jo.

13 January. Satellite phone.

Jo: Maria's got a dreadful cold.

Me: Is she with you?

Jo: Yes, she's been here a few days. She'll stay here until she's better.

15 January. Skype.

Jo, his head inclined, held in his hand, with a pale, inscrutable gaze: Kindergartens! Now Maria and I are both laid up with this bug that's going round.

Me: So, isn't she with Gry now?

Jo runs two fingers over his brow, averts his gaze towards the edge of the screen: Gry's very busy with a big project at work. We've agreed that Maria's better off with me for now.

Me: That means you'll have to postpone your journey?

Jo, looking straight at me, biting his lower lip: Yes.

17 January. Satellite phone.

Me: I miss you.

Jo: I miss you too. But it's impossible to abandon Maria with things as they are right now.

19 January. Skype.

Me: So, when d'you think you'll come?

Jo puts a hand over his mouth, pinches his chin: I'll have to wait and see. But all being well, I expect to leave some time at the beginning of February.

On the day after that conversation, in the grey morning light, when the new moon hangs in the sky like a fishing hook being lowered into the ocean, I see a flock of birds swoop in from the east and land on the fjord in front of the cabin. I grab my binoculars and zoom in on them. King eiders. I focus on one of the males, easily recognizable by the orange bump on its forehead and the crimson beak. I follow their movements from my window as they glide back and forth before suddenly diving and disappearing into the water for minutes at a time. I barely remember to breathe, utterly transfixed by them. I know their visit will be brief; they will fatten themselves up in the fjords before returning to the Siberian tundra to nest by freshwater lakes. I watch them with a sharp sense of loss. Or hunger. A change in the sea temperature will mean a change in the prey fauna.

High Arctic species will be driven further north, while new, warmth-loving species will push in from the south. We may not see king eiders here in the future. There may not be enough food for them in the ocean's depths.

I want to go out, to see, to hear this flock of birds, but I'm not sure I'll make it. They might fly off before I'm ready. I put down my binoculars, grab my scooter suit from the hook, shove my legs and arms into it, and my feet into my boots, and then I dash out, stomping over snow, stepping through paper-thin layers of ice, and make it down to the shore, where I find a viewing point among the rocks and seaweed from which to stare and listen.

Between the gentle lapping and thunderous roar of the waves, I can hear their cries. The males' deep vibrating whoops.

Haooh, haooh.

I look. Listen.

There are so many answers. And so many questions that are never asked.

14

On one of these January days, as I sit and ponder the colours in the sky, I think about perception and the sense of sight. I consider those episodes in which I see Borghild and Olaf. I find myself thinking of them as electrons in the mysterious world of quantum mechanics. Electrons jumping from one orbit to another, releasing, with each leap closer to the nucleus, energy in the form of light. Light of varying wavelengths, each emitting a distinctive colour. Electrons that only become manifest when they collide with something else, just like myself and Borghild and Olaf. Just as quantum mechanics cannot describe *what* is happening, only *how* one physical entity is observed by another, I cannot explain why these images are so vivid. All I can do is recount my daydreams, the things I imagine with such clarity. For example, the fire out here in the bay more than 140 years ago. I have concluded that it happened exactly like this:

It is a bitterly cold winter's night. The children, six in all, have gone up to the attic and settled in bed, their clothes still on beneath woollen blankets and sheepskin covers. That night the two-year-old Niels sleeps up there too, even though he's not yet weaned and might get restless and wake up. He's been known to get up from the foot of his parents' bench, where he usually sleeps, and wander half asleep into the kitchen, then through the cabin to the hot stove. Luckily his father has always discovered him on these little adventures across the floor. The stove is Olaf's domain at night. He is the one who gets up to add more logs and who, in the coldest hours, keeps the fire going from the bench. Normally, he tucks Niels in next to his mother on the inside of the bed and sits at its foot until he falls back to sleep. Tonight, however, Olaf is not at home. He is at a trading post further south, so the stove and fire will be Borghild's responsibility. She thinks it's best for the boy to sleep upstairs, with the warmth of his big sisters.

The windowpane at the end of the narrow room where the children sleep is covered with ice, and frost peeps out from the moss in the gaps in the log walls, like thick crusts of icing sugar. The scant heat flows along the stove's iron chimney, which goes from the ground floor up to the attic. As in most simple dwellings, the cold seeps in and heat leaks out. Timbers, like people, stiffen and shrink in the frost.

Olaf has told Borghild to be cautious when stoking the fire, vigilant as always about everything on the farm. But in her opinion he is too sparing with the wood. When the temperature outside drops, it gets far too cold. In his absence, and with the boy upstairs, she adds extra fine, dry birch wood several times, until the iron rings on the hot plate glow a fiery red. Then she does as he does, settles on the bench, fully dressed, her head resting on a rolled-up cloth, hands folded under her cheek and her attention turned sleepily towards the stove.

Night twinkles over the house and the bird cliff. The stove crackles, the log walls and floorboards creak, and a soft sigh moves through the woodwork, through the children in their trundle beds, past her on the bench, and in the background, beneath it all, is the eternal booming of the sea. Sounds ebb and flow, harmonious and discordant, a symphony on whose surface she floats for a while, until, increasingly heavy and drowsy, she sinks into it and sleeps.

It is the screams of her second-oldest daughter that break through. Smoke is seeping into the room! Borghild is instantly on her feet, and as she heads for the staircase she hears her own screams mingle with the screams and commotion up in the attic; she sees the smoke curling out from around the stove, up towards the ceiling and floor above, and deep in the soot-black waves, a spark that suddenly bursts into flame. She screams again. Grabs the bucket of water and throws it over the stove. The window, she shouts. You must open the window and jump out! Coughing, her eyes streaming, she struggles to the stairs and starts to climb, step by step, until the flames and smoke make her throat and her lungs sting and, unable to breathe, she retreats and collapses onto the floor. Down there, in the layer of clear air, she can recognize objects and manages to orientate herself. She crawls past the table legs, past the underside of the bench and on towards the front door, then, after fumbling with the handle briefly, she flings it open.

She is greeted by a vast, liberating expanse of white. The cold air is like a blessing, but as she gets to her feet she hears a terrible sound, like the roar of an injured animal. She turns. The house, their home, is ablaze, engulfed in flames, a fire so hot, so enormous, it is as though the Devil himself had sought refuge inside.

Is everyone here? she yells out to the children, her voice barely audible over the sound of the flames as they devour dry planks and timbers. They seem to appear from all directions and from the deepest dark, her angels, their faces black with soot. Two are bleeding from cuts on their foreheads and hands, another is limping. They cling to one another, sobbing. She stretches out a trembling hand. Counts them. Once. Twice. Asks again in that voice that refuses to carry: Niels. My baby boy. Where is he?

I cry with her as I sit here at the other end of the 140 years that divide us. I too feel loss. The loss of something as simple as Lina's sweet breath against my cheek, the tickle of her wispy hair, the weight of her little body in my arms. I have felt this loss every single day out here. And yet I can never really comprehend her loss, any more than I can understand Jo when he talks with such certainty about Maria. The sum of his experience can never encompass what I feel I have lost. Perhaps that is what these imaginative creations of mine really are. Perhaps they are about an altogether different experience, pulled apart, reworked and dramatized into an unrecognizable version of true events.

*

For example:

The house S and I owned jointly had a small but sunny roof terrace. We could spend hours there, especially after Lina was born. In the winter we would sit well wrapped up in wicker chairs under the patio heater, looking at the trees and passers-by on the road beyond as the snow crumbled away and the light slowly returned. When the temperature rose and the midday sun hung directly above the terrace, we set up glass partitions, a little greenhouse, which we eventually expanded to accommodate two growing boxes. The terrace with its greenhouse became a place, a way, to be together. Lina slept well out in the fresh air and later, as she got bigger, it offered her a play area where she could toddle about with a small watering can in her hands, poke her fingers in the earth and watch seedlings grow into something edible, sweet or bitter, that she was allowed to put in her mouth.

During the last months before I left, I spent a lot of time out there, feeding the soil with compost and manure, sowing seeds, planting cuttings and seedlings, mostly to escape the tense atmosphere indoors, but also for Lina's sake. I wanted her life to go on as before.

By June, after much careful feeding and diligent watering, the salad leaves appeared from the earth, crisp and juicy. In the sunniest corner a tomato plant hung heavy with necklaces of green berries, and a courgette plant reached carefully over the edge of its pot with its voluminous, orange flowers. It had become mine, this greenhouse. Whatever grew there grew because I wanted it to. This was certainly how S viewed it – something I only fully appreciated after I came back from university one afternoon. Standing outside the front door were some large, very full, tightly knotted rubbish bags. Running through the house was a trail of sand and earth. My hand went up to my chest and I held it there, as though to remind myself to breathe, then I walked through the kitchen, out into the living room and towards the terrace door that had been left ajar. I stopped in the doorway, holding the door frame for support. All the plant pots and boxes had been overturned and emptied. Torn lettuce leaves were strewn floppy and pale over the flagstones, a courgette flower lay flattened, squashed under one of the glass partitions, and in the corner, dangling from a string, was one lonely, torn stem of a tomato plant. I stumbled out and sank into the wicker chair. I sat there until I heard the key in the front door, steps in the hallway, at which point I rose, got to my feet, ready to confront S. I restrained myself as soon as I saw him standing in the doorway with Lina in his arms. Seeing her put her arm around her father's neck, clinging to him tightly, turning away from me, wide-eyed and frightened, I wanted nothing but to soften the sight of such chaos and destruction. But before I could say a word, S pointed towards the wrecked pots and boxes and whispered, with his mouth close to Lina's cheek: Look, Lina. Look. At what Mummy has done to us.

15

Lina. My double me. What she breathes in, I breathe out. What she absorbs, she passes on to me. We are each other's heart and lungs, but also each other's shadow. Is it myself I see in her, or she who sees herself in me?

Our oldest mountain is 2,900 million years old and lies in the very north of the country. Here too Lina and I have a piece of our history, and of those 2,900 million years our ages so far are thirty-six and three respectively. Those 2,900 million years are marked by various events: collisions of continents, volcanic eruptions, falling asteroids and the slow grinding of glaciers. The enormity of the time represented by these mountains takes my breath away. The few seasons that Lina and I spend together will have hardly any impact on the mountain's structure or surface, and when I stood there, in front of S with my arms stretched out to Lina, fearful of not reaching something or other *in time*, a single sentence entered my mind, with which I comforted myself: This is nothing, nothing in the greater scheme of things.

16

So many answers. So many questions never asked.

Whenever I stand in the bay or drive across the plateau, they seem to be everywhere. The things I don't know. Or quite understand. The wind and weather, the sea and sky. The seabirds and their migration towards their colonies. I know yet do not know. And I sometimes think the same about myself and my own life. S and I, for example. How it happened. There were two of us. And Lina. It had once been good, before it got difficult and painful. Situations and events that gave me reason to pause, things he did or did not do. My desire to explain away his reactions, his way of being. Seeing his anger as evidence of something genuine and instinctive. His silence as a sign of calm and sensitivity. His stubbornness as proof of determination and strong character.

I pointed them out and praised them. But he sought to drain any meaning from the characteristics I attributed to him. He muddied himself, so to speak, until there wasn't a single bright spot to be seen. Until he was left with only the traits that he chose to show: anger, irrationality, an inability to express himself.

But even before that he was a riddle: he carried a thousand answers within him, if only I could find the right questions. I searched for clues in the entire length of his spine, as he lay there at night, and in his eyes when he returned from work. In the music he played, the films he watched, the books he read. In his smell in the bedding, his shirts, his jeans, in the wet towels he would leave on the bathroom floor after he'd had a shower. I examined, sniffed, breathed him in, but he left no impression, no sign that might lead me further, and so I failed to find the questions, the hints, that might, like a magic formula, open him up.

Wasn't I doing things right? Wasn't I curious enough? Empathic enough? I certainly tried my best.

For example:

In the evenings, I'd watch him at the kitchen counter making food, his back stooped, an impenetrable look on his face. Then I would observe him as he wandered around the house with a faraway gaze. I sensed that there was a void within him, a vacuum of such magnitude that his frame, his very being, was in danger of crashing down in a silent implosion. Sometimes I felt his absence so intensely that it made me feel almost dizzy. Nonetheless, I would sit next to him on the sofa, as close as his boundaries would allow. I might place a hand on his thigh, rest my head cautiously on his shoulder, manoeuvre myself, sneak towards an intimacy that creaked and teetered and shivered, until I was able to ask questions and tease out answers.

I might say:

Hey, I get the feeling something's wrong.

Hey, I can sense you're unhappy.

Hey, has something happened?

Hey, what's up?

You can tell me what it is.

And he'd answer:

Hmm.

I've no idea what you're talking about.

No.

I don't know.

It's nothing.

It was my perception. I was the one who saw him this way. That's what I might sometimes think later. That this lack of depth, this deficit, what happened on that sofa, was not within him. Instead it was my own emptiness reflected.

17

Male and female seabirds both sit on the eggs. Neither one abandons the nest, no matter how harsh the conditions in the colony. I witnessed it myself as a student during fieldwork on a kittiwake cliff. That spring the nesting site was hit by a violent storm that covered the ledges and the kittiwakes' nests with thick, heavy snow, until each nest was in a capsule of tightly packed ice. They sat inside for days, without moving. From where I was, studying the phenomenon through my binoculars, the only signs of life were their beaks poking out of the snow.

Once the eggs have hatched, the parents continue to share their duties. While one tends the nest, the other flies out to fetch food for themselves and the chicks. They continue like this, twenty-four hours a day, flying back and forth, feeding the chicks, who eat vast quantities and grow quickly. Both parents stay with the chicks until they are big enough to fly the nest. In the case of kittiwakes this is at about six weeks; gannets take a whole thirteen. Razorbills and guillemots reach a clear division of responsibility when their chicks are about three weeks old: while still tiny and not yet adept at flying, the little chicks leave the nest and their mother to follow their father in a perilous leap from the cliffs. Those who survive complete their development out on the ocean with him alone.

I may be thinking about the seabirds, their breeding success and stock sizes, but it is S and Lina, Jo and Maria whom I see. And then, just as an electron leaps from one orbit to another, it is Olaf and Niels whom I see. Olaf's bond with Niels, Niels's bond with Olaf, the relationship between the two of them as it played out in the time they had together.

Borghild observed it clearly when the boy was about six months old. One spring day she and Olaf were in the shed after shearing. She was engrossed in sorting the wool to be cleaned and carded, while he was feeding the newly shorn sheep with fresh grass, spreading it over the stall with a pitchfork. Suddenly he stopped, stood and listened before putting down his pitchfork with a distant expression. The boy's crying, he said, shooting a glance at her. Yes, he must be hungry, she replied, wiping her hands on her apron, greasy with lanolin from the wool. Before she had time to gather herself, he was out of the shed, leaving her bewildered and staring after him, and at the specks of dust that swirled in the light from the open door. She shook her head and stuffed a stray lock of hair under her scarf. It was clear that Olaf was besotted by the boy. She went over to the doorway, aware of the hum of her daughters' play. The crying had now stopped, and as a warm ray of sun swept over her she registered a sadness, but also a sense of relief. At last Olaf had the son he had so ardently wished for. It was only reasonable and right that he now show his tenderness for the boy. He had been a good father to the girls thus far, but it was to her they usually turned.

She went in. Olaf was sitting on a stool by the cradle, rocking it back and forth, while Niels stared wide-eyed at his father from his pillow. She picked up the little boy without a word, settled on the bench and put him to her breast. He was hungry and fed greedily, but as soon as he was satisfied he turned back to his father with a smile and she buttoned up her bodice. As she got up to put him back in his cradle, Olaf came towards her with outstretched hands and, taking the boy gently from her arms, he settled back on the stool with him in the crook of his arm.

It would go on like this for the two years that Niels lived. It was Olaf who took the boy out with him to the shed, whether to chop wood or feed the animals. Olaf who let the boy be present for the gutting of fish, the mending of nets or the grinding of axes, sickles and knives. Olaf who took him out on little trips as soon as he could walk, who insisted that Niels should witness the slaughter despite being so young. And it was Olaf who was so keen that the boy should follow whatever he did, that Niels should call up to him when he climbed under the eaves to hang the salted mutton out to dry.

Niels repaid his father's attentions with a devotion that glowed in his plump cheeks. By the age of one he was tottering about with sawdust on the seat of his trousers and fish blood on his fingers. Lord help us, Borghild might exclaim, but she did not intervene. The boy would clearly learn to take responsibility early under his father's gentle, observant gaze. It couldn't be denied that this suited her. She had enough to do. And perhaps this made Olaf bind Niels to him even more strongly. She wasn't attentive enough, he might sometimes say, and it seemed now and then that he would have liked the boy to himself.

This was doubtless what Borghild thought about in her grief when she mourned for Niels later. The unexpected significance he'd had for Olaf. After the boy's birth, this place and their work here, life itself, had gained a meaning she hadn't realized Olaf hankered after.

Was that how it was?

I am spinning a story out of thin air and my own experiences. Am I stretching it too far?

18

It is S who has custody of Lina. It is S who looks after her so steadfastly, so attentively, who provides her with food, comfort and love, who tucks her in at bedtime. That's obvious, it goes without saying, when I'm away all these months. And that's what I tell myself too. It would have been impossible to have Lina with me out here. The unpredictable weather, the trips to the bird cliff, the weeks of solitude, cut off from the outside world. I wouldn't have got any work done, not for a moment.

That's the obvious truth. But like many of the truths in our life, S's and mine, it is distorted. I handed Lina over to him, surrendered care and control, without protest, without objection, not just in an attempt to buy myself out of guilt, or on account of his behaviour, the countless alarming episodes, but because of the direct threats:

S: If you take Lina, I'll take you.

S: If I get her, I might just leave you alone.

S: I know you, your vulnerable spots.

S: I'll find you both, whatever.

*

I'm sitting at the plank table, studying the latest measurements that I've downloaded from the data logger and the research buoy in the sea. It is dark in the cabin. The only light source is my PC, a rectangular blue-white light that streams out into the room, drawing me to it like the gateway to a secret sanctuary. I am forced to ask myself the question or, to be more precise, to acknowledge why I find myself in such a remote place, so far away from people and civilization.

I've hidden myself. That's what I've done. Dug myself in like a squealing rat, in fear of his rage, the force of the words he threatened me with. Words that made my throat close up, my breathing stop, long before he could hit me physically. I can't deny it. Yes, my research is driven by ambition, a desire to reach the goals I've set myself, but I have ploughed ahead with it so quickly and so completely because I felt compelled to come up with a plausible reason to get away. I needed a firm plan that might calm him down. The funding was in place. Six months' planning time was all I required. And now here I am. Out of S's panoptic gaze and hopefully out of his mind. But for how long?

It's so dark, so dark in here. I switch on the wall lamps. The light over the cooker. The darkness is like earth: I dig deeper until I reach the place that, by daylight, in the weightless translucency of things, I rarely or never come close to. Shivering with cold, I rub my arms. If only the truth were unalterable. Unambiguous and fixed. But like emotions, the truth has no yardstick. No fixed value. It oscillates, changes direction and colour, and right now it is split, defined by goals and intentions. It is rooted in my own completely subjective feelings. Yet the truth is also this: I have freed up some room, cleared a space for Jo and myself. A nest where we can fuck and love, disappear into a contourless, all-consuming sphere, without any interference, confrontation or disturbance, far, far away from S, who doesn't know, hasn't the slightest idea about my underlying plan and secret reward.

19

While I am waiting, I occasionally push myself to my limits. Evening, afternoon or morning, I can suddenly fling on my clothes, fill the scooter with petrol and drive right out into the white nothingness. Thighs tight around the seat, thumb pressed firmly on the accelerator, I ride over the snowdrifts and snow dunes so fast that the machine roars and shakes under me, until I take off and fly weightless through the air, unsure for a second or two where or how I will land. Then I surrender, sweating, with my heart pounding.

Just hours later, I might go into the shed, drag out a sack of wood and stand, legs wide apart, in front of the chopping block with the axe in my hands. I set the blade in the first log, raise my arms, split it into ever smaller pieces. And so I continue, arms up, then down hard, rhythmic, almost meditative. I watch the axe glide through each log, tearing the wood like an old hunk of dried meat, until the bag is empty and I am surrounded by chips of wood spread like sawdust in a circus ring.

Sometimes, in the fragile daylight that is gathering strength day by day, I stand outside the cabin and scream.

Facing the shore and fjord, I hunch over, draw in as much icy air as I can and then, with muscles tensed and fists clenched, I push out the air, making the deepest and also the highest sounds I can. I empty myself utterly and completely of voice and energy, but also of rage. I release a power, a storm from within, which spreads out across the bay and fjord, followed by an astonishing but absolute silence, convincing me for an instant that I can govern not just myself but also other people, and perhaps even nature itself.

I govern myself to the nth degree. In the evenings, under my duvet, I stoke up my desire, satisfying each thought that drifts my way until I shake with ecstasy. I stink of petrol, frying oil and sweat. My arm and neck muscles bulge, I see it in the mirror in the kitchen. I am brimming with power, with a will for self-governance so strong that I decide one day to read the text from S, fourteen days after I received it.

I will read it late in the evening, so I can head straight to bed afterwards. I know I will be exhausted. From being obliged to let him in. Seeing his words spread across the screen, addressing themselves directly at me. Exhausted, no matter how simple or unambiguous the message might be.

I sit on the edge of the bed and stare into the display, the blue force field that draws me in like the entrance to an underworld. I open my inbox, then his text. Just one sentence. Short. It strikes me that I have heard and read it many times before, in alternative versions: *Never believe you are beyond my reach.*

20

I watch the moon's changing phases, from new moon to full moon, from pitch darkness to shiny silver with sharp divisions of light and shade. The moon is waning when I wake up early one morning with a feeling of pressure in my abdomen. I recognize it of course, this pressure, it's to be expected. Yesterday evening I found a brown stripe in my knickers, so before going to bed I put on a sanitary pad – well prepared, I thought – in case the bleeding got heavier overnight. I lie for a while feeling the sense of weight in my pelvis, of being bloated and sponge-like, from my navel all the way round to the small of my back. I shift carefully, and then I feel it, the dreaded trickle down my perineum, a steady ooze that spreads onto the pad, but also between my buttocks, where the blood might run down the back of my knickers and leak onto my bedclothes. I clamp my legs together and swing them over the edge of the bed. Then, with a hand firmly on my crotch, I tiptoe awkwardly across the floor of my sleeping alcove, through the living area and to the front door, which in my haste I slam against the wall, before with bare feet I take the three or four steps over the snow to the privy. Oh my God, what a mess. I make a grab for the loo paper, stuff it between my legs, wipe myself as best I can, before I sit down with a sigh on the polystyrene toilet seat and let the liquid run over the icy pool beneath me. I soon feel the frost nipping painfully at my toes and thighs, but despite my discomfort I have to put my feet back on the freezing-cold floor, get up and wipe myself again with masses of paper, as I hop from one foot to the other to stay warm. When at last I get a square of paper with no visible trace of blood, I fling open the privy door ready to dash back in, but I stop, rigid with terror, even though I know exactly what I am looking at. The flecks of blood in the snow, in an arc from the front door to the outside toilet, resemble the ominous traces of a fight. As if a badly injured man has fled through one door and hidden behind another. There's something dramatic about these droplets of my blood, and I consider leaving them until they are erased in the natural way, by my own footprints or the next fall of snow.

21

22 January. The sun hangs plump and resplendent on the edge of the horizon, a blaze of yellow spilling out of the sky and over the fjord like melted butter. A sunny day. Hurrah! From now on the sun will continue to climb, until come mid-May it will stay in the sky for months on end. I am standing outside the cabin, drinking in the light across the isthmus, where the sharp cliffs and soft slopes sparkle and glitter and twinkle. A sight, an event that has to be celebrated with fresh fish.

The waters are too shallow along the shore here, but further south is a headland that juts out over the deep waters of the fjord. I drive across the bay, park close to a rock face, grab my fishing rod and climb the craggy slopes up to the furthest point, the perfect place from which to fish. The waters are calmer here than at the bird cliff, which is open to the ocean. Nevertheless, the waves are choppy and seem to lick and snap at the headland with salty, thirsty tongues. I cast my line and reel it in, cast it and reel it in. I have the sun at my back and the fjord before me, open, expansive and naked. The land on the other side is scarcely visible.

The only life here is the water that heaves and pounds against the rocks, gurgling like a gigantic, formless animal. It seems to want to test its strength, challenge me to a fight, and for a moment I feel exposed, infinitely alone, as indeed I am. But only minutes after this thought, I feel a tug on my fishing rod.

I haul in three small fjord cod in quick succession, then call it a day. With my catch unhooked, one fist around their abdomens, the other round their gills, I break their necks one by one, fling them onto the hard, grainy snow, and there they lie, their smooth, glossy skins reflecting the sunlight, jerking now and then with a last convulsion, blood trickling from their mouths. I squat down, take my knife from its sheath, slice through the belly with the tip, pull out the guts that spill between my fingers, then, digging deeper behind the gills, I tear the last of the innards loose.

As I focus on gutting the first fish I hear a hoarse scream above me. A black-backed gull. Where did it come from? There wasn't a single bird in sight while I was fishing. I gut the next two fish: knife in, intestines out. As I get up and slip the knife back in its sheath, I hear it again, the screeching, but this time from three or four gulls. They circle right over me with their sharp beaks, beat their wings hungrily, and then one of them swoops down, straight at me, snatching a sliver of gut that stretches out into a long, thin string before swerving out over the fjord as it tries to gulp down its prize. All at once there's a wild commotion of flapping and screeching. Several gulls are squabbling over the spoils. Five or six more black-backs have arrived and are now circling over me, greedy for the innards I'm about to throw into the sea. I feel the power, standing in a pool of fish blood with this carrion in my hands. I get a thrill out of the gulls' keen-eyed vigilance, the way they fly closer, ready to throw themselves on the prey if I so much as shake my wrist. I tease the birds a couple of times before finally launching the strips of intestines, laughing out loud as I watch them sail through the air, the sky thickening with hooked beaks and scraggy claws. Always ready, I think, and laugh again, loudly and shrilly, in a bid to assert myself, to take my rightful place: a human voice, strong and penetrating, rising above their jabbering animal screeches.

I thread the three cod onto a stick, pick up my rod and leave, turning several times to stare back at the lunch party in the sky, then walk on, as the gulls' cries gradually subside. Embarking on my climb down the steep slope, I turn one last time, but the sky is as empty and vast now as the silence of the gulls. I focus on my descent and to make it easier I transfer my fishing rod to the same hand as my catch, holding it upright before me, while my feet search for firm ground.

Suddenly I feel a blow to my shoulder and slip as though I've been pushed. There's a tugging on the fishing rod in my hand followed by a ripping sound, and there, high above me, I see the line unreel and stretch out in an arc, thin and light as a spider's thread on a summer's day, before it tumbles straight at me with the hook at its head. I feel a sting, a pain in my cheek, and then, without at first seeing any connection, I realize that the fishing rod has hooked itself onto something. I pull on it and, bewildered, with blood pumping from my cheek, I feel the skin pull away, and then the ground beneath me loosens, I lurch towards the edge, lose my balance and fall.

I fall through the air, not far, two or three metres perhaps. But as I fall I remember a phenomenon I witnessed some years ago, during a field trip near a kittiwake mountain further south. There was fog that day, thick and fleecy, like newly washed sheep's wool wrapped around the mountain that towered out of the sea, covered with kittiwake nests on every shelf and ledge. I was lying on my stomach on an outcrop below them with a periscope in my hand, trying to put a data logger into one of the nests to measure the temperature, but the fog was making it almost impossible. All around and above me I could hear life bustling, the screaming and flapping of kittiwakes flying to and from the mountain. It is this I think of as I fall. The amazing phenomenon that these birds could navigate with such precision. That they knew exactly where they were going as they broke through the fog and flew straight onto their nests.

22

The waves, the heartbeat of the sea, roll into the shore and out again, back and forth in a steady rhythm, sometimes in perfect time with my own heartbeat and sometimes out of step. Lulled and rocked to sleep like a child, completely at one with my surroundings, I sleep deeply and I sleep long. It is almost morning when I open my eyes.

The pale glow of the wall lamps in the living area is visible through a chink in the dividing curtain. The generator is on and the familiar sound of wood crackling issues cheerfully from the stove. The cabin is warm and it's so snug under the duvet, so lovely and comfortable, that all I want is to do is to go on dozing. I stretch and yawn. But instantly stiffen. An intense and searing pain grips my ankle. I can barely open my mouth because the skin from my jaw to my temples is throbbing so painfully. I touch my face and prop myself up in bed. I sit for a moment and stare out into the room, confused, then gather myself and heave the bedclothes aside. My ankle is bandaged. With care. With precision. And under my fingertips, I feel the surface of a plaster that extends from my jaw to my nose. I check my watch, close my eyes tight shut, concentrating, trying to remember what happened. The gulls, the fishing, the catch, this all comes back to me clearly, my climbing down the slope and then falling. I touch my head, rub my brow. But this. That I've driven back from the headland to the cabin. Looked after my wound. Bandaged my ankle. Put wood in the stove. No, I've no memory of that at all. It's as though it's been erased. Blanked out.

I put one foot down on the floor. Try to stand on both, but again this goddamn pain. Fucking hell, I yell. Bent double, so as not to put weight on my ankle, I shuffle out of the sleeping alcove, stand between the kitchen and living area and look around. Nothing unusual, apart from a faint fishy smell. I turn and find a serving dish on the kitchen counter, filled with cod, cut into chunks. I limp over to it, poke my finger into the flesh: just as I thought, poached and ready to serve. I continue, more purposefully, into the living area, open the front door. The scooter is parked where it should be, on the spot I cleared of snow. I slam the door and stand there, puzzled, motionless, until I slump onto a chair by the table with my head in my hands. I sit there, lost in speculation over the events of the last twenty-four hours, until the cold sneaks under my thermal underwear and I become aware of a glimmer of daylight on the horizon. Or is it my satellite phone on the windowsill that draws my attention? The icon in the right-hand corner that indicates an unread message?

It's from Jo. I read it, aware of the look of astonishment on my face, corroborated by my reflection in the window when I glance up. I concentrate again and reread the message, but I still can't quite grasp what it's referring to: *Good that you're managing for now. Get well soon!*

I let out a strangled cry. And as I try to make a connection between the words and my sense of confusion when I woke up, I watch my thumbs, as though from far outside myself, flit over the keys and open the text messages which seem to have passed between us, five in all, between ten and eleven last night:

Me: *Had an accident. Fishing hook in my cheek. Sprained ankle. All good.*

Jo: *Poor you. How did it happen?*

Me: *Cod fishing. Fell down a cliff.*

Jo: *How's it going? Do you need help?*

Me: *No, I'm fine. Back on my feet in a day or two.*

I've no recollection of writing these words, nor for that matter of walking about with my phone, searching for a connection, either outside or in. How did I manage it with this pain in my foot? It can't have been me. Perhaps I've not been myself. A funny turn or loss of consciousness, that's what I've had. I try to console myself with this, to buoy myself up, as a disturbing tingle rises up my spine. I clutch the back of my neck, rotate my shoulders as though to liberate myself physically from my anguish. For a moment I want to cry – my jaw judders, my eyes well up – but on the next breath I take control of myself by biting down hard on my knuckles. If I'm to stay here, I cannot give way to fantasies about unmeasurable events. I fell. Suffered a loss of memory. That's all there is to it. That's it.

23

I lie beneath the duvet, thrashing around in an ice-cold sea, trying to cling to one of the ice floes that are drifting about. I grab the edge of one, but as soon as I start to pull myself onto it, it tips over and I lose my grip and glide back into the water. I want to try again as another ice floe heads my way, bigger this time, but it rushes towards me at speed and rams into my head with a thud.

I wake up, freezing cold and drenched in sweat. The moaning sound I heard, the dreadful wailing, did it come from my dream or from somewhere in the cabin? I lie there paralysed, heavy and motionless, until I feel a powerful heartbeat and a tingling sensation spread from my chest into my limbs. The mouse in the kitchen cupboard, I really must kill it once and for all, because now I hear its tiny footsteps crossing the floor, claws scraping against the wooden boards, alternately sharp and soft. Or is someone sitting at the table writing? Is it a pen on paper I hear?

No, I don't like it. Lying here like this, listening to my surroundings. I have a fever. My senses are as fragile as thin glass, the light is too sharp, the sounds too loud, the bed-clothes too rough. I'm shivering, I've got goosebumps and

I feel horribly shaky. It's hard work, feeling my imagination wreak havoc in this feverish body. Even the cupboards and walls seem to stare back at me with expectant faces. And now I can hear it again, the sound of moaning, albeit weaker this time. Is it coming from me or the stove? Is it just the embers dying? The logs collapsing and turning to ash?

I fix my gaze on the ceiling. Force my thoughts out onto the open sea, to the North-West Atlantic and the stretch of sea between Newfoundland and the mid-Atlantic. Where the kittiwakes are now wintering until March or April, and where, far from dry land in the modest gap between sunrise and sunset, they swoop over vast areas hunting for food, for herrings, sprats, capelins and krill. I want to think about concrete, logical problems, such as the consequences of the rise in sea temperatures, acidification, the increase in parasites and changes in the nutrient base. Conditions that might prevent the birds from returning to the colony, from nesting, from increasing their population. But I regret not having asked Jo for help. That he didn't realize for himself that it's time he should come now, here to me. This helplessness, I don't like it, and I pinch myself very hard.

24

The cabin is freezing cold. A blizzard hurls itself against the log walls. It is impossible to see out of the little window above my bed, with the windblown snow lying thick against the pane. I sink into my bed. Pull the duvet up over me. All I can do again is wait. For the storm to abate and the snow to ease. For the bacteria that are coursing through in my bloodstream to be defeated and the fever to recede.

Two storms, two battles. Hours in stand-off. It's more than enough for one person. I can feel my fortifications crumbling as I lie here, then I'm off again. Defenceless. I allow myself to be swept along by a stream of images that quickly break down all reason, all the figures and statistics that I have so carefully built up as a dam against the thoughts to which I now so easily succumb. First, I see the faces of Lina and S, then Jo's, Maria's, Gry's. Gestures and expressions, fragmented actions and scenes that float about like twigs on the surface of water before being sucked, in a maelstrom, to my very core, where they get stuck and begin to build up, until I spill over with tears and lie quietly like still, algae-green water.

A gap opens up, a liberating breath, but just as I'm finally dozing off I am woken by a question that falls through me like a stone. I sit up in bed, repeat the question, quietly whisper to myself: How could I?

How could you? shouts Olaf again, slamming his fist into the table so hard that its wooden legs rasp against the earth floor. How could you stoke up the fire like that? And why in the world did you let him sleep with the girls? You knew the boy needed watching!

Borghild flinches under the tirade of questions, clenches her fists so as not to break down under the weight of Olaf's fury. He doesn't need to repeat it. For months she has tortured herself for her carelessness. The excessive wood burning. Her mistake in allowing the little one to sleep upstairs with his sisters. But faced with his anger she goes into lockdown and retreats into herself. She cannot allow herself to take on the full brunt of his condemnation. How, then, could the two of them live together? And the girls certainly can't be blamed. All five older but not old enough for the responsibility that was given to them so disastrously that night. Each thought one of the other sisters was looking after him. Besides, who sees whom with flames licking at their hair and clothes and feet? It was a matter of getting out before they themselves were burned to death.

They sit in a mud hut, each on their own stool around the hearth. A temporary shelter, somewhere to stay until the new house is completed on the site of the fire. Olaf's burst of rage has subsided and a sense of relief comes over Borghild. After a while they both sit with their hands folded in prayer and give thanks for the help they have had from people in the villages further into the fjord, all those who have provided food, clothes, utensils and tools, the transportation of new and dry timbers. And not least, they give thanks for their children. The lives that God allowed them to keep. But when their prayers are over Olaf can't restrain himself. Stooping under the low ceiling, he stares out of the small window, at the new building that is going up, and whispers hoarsely: To think what you've wrecked. And without another word he goes out to the work that awaits him. Everything that could be said has been said. Forcibly. Many times over.

She goes to the window and watches the wind tug at his shirt, sneak in over his shoulders and down the hollow of his back, which is outlined by little patches of sweat. She watches him as he is drawn reluctantly, as though by some invisible force, towards the white timbers, the new logs which he has notched into the foundation wall that still stands on the fire site. He is walking, she thinks, towards what will soon be a similar but strangely alien house.

She misses his arms about her. Here in the mud hut they sleep in separate beds. Nor does he ever look for her in the shed, unless something practical needs doing. She gets up, straightens her scarf, opens the door and steps out into the spring light, which is sharp and piercing, like a scream, she thinks. She gathers her skirts and crosses the clearing in long strides, over the grass that pokes through the patches of wet snow. Breathless, she approaches the new building, and the man who has his back turned and an axe in his fist. She touches his shoulder, and when he looks round his eyes are wide. The look of an animal, she thinks, wild, bordering on mad, like the farm dog they once had. She stretches out a hand towards him, both hands, but they hang clumsily in the space between them. She notices it and quickly lets them drop.

Little clouds with creamy tops drift across the sky, while light and shade flutter over green shoots and year-old tufts of grass that bend in the wind now and then. A screeching of gulls, a bleating of sheep, the voices of girls at play, and here she stands, without purpose, her throat and mouth tinder-dry, as though filled with the ash that still lies inside the foundation walls. All the words she wants to say, she struggles to get them out. Or perhaps they fly out, like the wind here, always giving the impression of haste?

Again. It is I, I, and nobody else who must speak. It is I who ought to explain, I who ought to ask myself questions.

I sit hunched up in bed, hands over my face. The storm rages about me. It whips and beats at the cabin walls, so they shudder and shake deep into the frozen ground. Or is it a still, clear day, with warm, sparkling sunshine over the isthmus? Is it only here in my alcove that everything seems to seethe and boil, in me that the wind is blowing at twenty-seven metres per second? I peer out into the room between my fingers. It is as though they were standing there by the dividing curtain, he and she, glaring at me as they glared at each other, awaiting self-knowledge, the question I have yet to ask myself. I put my hands over my ears, because it's coming now, the question, and I might as well yell it out, since nobody else can hear it anyway: How the hell could I? How could I leave Lina?

25

25 January, eleven o'clock.

Wind: twenty-seven metres per second.

According to the Beaufort scale, storm, whole gale, force ten. Very high waves with long overhanging crests. Dense patches of sea foam are blown in the direction of the wind, the whole surface of the sea takes on a white appearance, and visibility is affected. According to the Norwegian Meteorological Institute, people should not venture out in this or any stronger winds. Trees may fall onto telephone wires and power cables. Timber walls creak. Small, lightly built houses are torn from their foundations.

29 January, eleven o'clock.

Wind: one point five metres per second.

According to the Beaufort scale, force one, light air. Breeze that can barely be felt. Drifting snowflakes indicate the wind direction.

*

My transition to a fever-free state coincides with high pressure. Until alternative explanations are available, I will allow the Meteorological Institute's descriptions to form the basis for the report on my emotional state.

26

The light, gentle wind strokes my fingers that hold the phone and moves carefully over the flaps of my sheepskin hat, which are hitched up for the occasion. It is as though it seeks forgiveness for its violent outburst and the havoc it wreaked the day before yesterday. It breathes softly on the snow heaped around the masts, barely rotating the anemometer and gently turning the wind vane in a south-easterly direction. I hear the dialling tone ring once, twice, and hope that Jo will take my call, that he'll be happy and welcoming, despite our agreement to call outside set times only when something unexpected occurs. I've been debating it myself: the four bars of signal visible on the display are certainly an unexpected event, unexpected enough, an irresistibly tempting opportunity to make contact. The conditions are optimal *now*, but won't be in a couple of hours.

I sink down on the edge of a snow dune, exhausted but satisfied. Something else I want to share with him: I've managed to repair the weather station after the storm, albeit with difficulty as I hobbled around with the murmuring echo of a fever still in my blood. The mast, which was leaning precariously over a snow dune, is securely tethered again, and I have replaced the old wind gauge, which seems to have vanished into the sea. Just imagine, Jo, I want to say, I managed all this, completely on my own.

He isn't answering, and as I hear the steady pulse of the dialling tone against my ear, my gaze wanders between the mast and the sensors on the weather station. A high-tech steel device that sucks up the language of the atmosphere, right here, right now, at three o'clock on 29 January. A godlike installation which, with the help of its tentacles, transforms the ancient weather gods' wrath and mercy into low and high pressure, which when measured digitally in hectopascals will contribute to a unified prediction of climate change.

I think of myself in relation to Jo. A wandering measuring device for his changes of mood, sensitive to distance and closeness and any communication disturbances, a sensory apparatus that via the electrical impulses of my neurons transforms his signals into one eternal, aching question: when are you coming?

Finally. A click and crackle and Jo's voice breaks through.

Jo: Hey, darling, what's going on?

Me: Everything and nothing, I just wanted to call. The conditions are optimal out here by the bird cliff today and I—

Jo: Ah, right… I was busy talking to the neighbouring office when I heard my phone ring and I got really worried when I realized it was you. Is everything OK?

Me: Everything's fine, except for my foot and the inflammation. Just wait till we Skype, my cheek's really swollen up.

Jo: Does that mean you've got worse and need help?

Me: No, not at all. I just wanted to tell you how happy I am that I've managed to fix the weather station and secure the mast again after the storm out here, and all with a foot that hurts like hell.

Jo: So everything's OK? I mean, you're calling because things—

Me: Yes, yes, everything's fine. I just had an impulse, that's all.

He hesitates for a second. I can imagine him looking stiffly at the floor, his front teeth biting into that plump lower lip, trying to make allowances for my breaking the deal, while reassuring himself that I'm not in a situation that will require him to abandon everything and come straight out here. He gathers himself. He is happy to hear my voice, I can tell by his warm tone as we go on talking – I about the storm, he about the situation back at home. The warmth drops by a few degrees when minutes later we move on to the subject of his arrival, of when I can expect to see him out here on the bay.

Jo: I'll be coming in three or four weeks.

Me: Three or four? A week ago you said the beginning of February.

Jo: I'd have come right away if I could, but I have to consider Gry. I'll have problems when I get back if I just go off for weeks without fitting my stay around her.

Me: Just go off? Surely you had this pretty much sorted with her when I left?

Jo: Gry's going through a hard time at work. And I don't want to hand Maria over to her with things as they are. Believe me, it's for Maria's sake. Not Gry's.

We try to round things off in an affectionate way. I whisper that I love him and he whispers back that he misses me, everything is fine, but as I say goodbye and send him a kiss, he slips it in…

Jo: We'll call at our scheduled times from now on, OK?

27

Jo knows full well that Gry is a problem. Just like S, but in the opposite way. Where S, beneath a veneer of self-sacrifice and duty, behaves so threateningly that I have to flee, Gry gives the impression of being so busy that it is difficult for Jo to find any time for his stay out here.

Gry sees herself as an entrepreneur and runs a company in the health sector. With five employees, the agency is regarded as such a success that even Jo defends her excessively long working hours. The everyday care of Maria falls largely to him, which he thinks best, as he doesn't trust Gry's judgement when things get hectic during the week. Wellies and changes of clothes when it's raining are easily forgotten, a high temperature can be overlooked, so to avoid the worry and calls from the kindergarten he prefers Maria to stay with him beyond the stipulated, evenly divided time.

I've met Gry on a few occasions. I can't say she made a huge impression, despite Jo's description of her as a visionary in her work and a woman who possesses a rare drive. To me, she seemed rather superficial and unrealistic, which might just explain the visionary word. I perceived her as totally different from me, and since we're also very different in appearance, I've never considered her to be a rival or a threat to my relationship with Jo. But by her sheer absence, her total preoccupation with her own life, she manages to push our relationship out of play and into a painful standby mode.

There's nothing more to say about Gry. That's it. She is, in herself, of little interest. But just as temperature and wind affect the breeding success of seabirds, she is a major cause of Jo's absence here at the bird cliff.

28

Days and nights come and go, twelve in all. Jo's not to be expected any time soon, but I am nevertheless due a visit. From the captain, the man responsible for bringing the supplies every five weeks. Since the first batch of supplies was calculated, in part, for two, I still have lots of provisions left on my shelves. However, I am excited about what's in the boxes, even though they've been filled according to my own precise instructions.

I stand at the mirror and inspect the wound on my cheek. The inflammation is still obvious: a yellow sausage of congealed pus lies like a stopper over the gash, and the skin around it is thin and puffy. It's not a difficult choice. If the sausage is to dry out properly and further irritation be prevented, my cheek mustn't be covered. I'll have to meet the captain as I am, with my infection exposed.

The exact time of his arrival is unspecified. The boat could appear on the fjord at any moment. There is work to do while it is still light, but I am distracted by the need to keep a lookout. I feel restless and tense, but also excited at the prospect of standing face to face with another human being at last, letting the talk rumble on, hearing another voice besides my own. I look forward to his physical presence, the weight of his being, a counterbalance to the diffuse, dreamlike quality which has filled this place for weeks now. I'll invite him in for coffee, of course, offer him something to eat. But, at the same time, I don't like the thought of appearing needy or weak in the eyes of a visiting stranger.

Later that afternoon, as I stand on the bird cliff transferring the readings onto my PC, I spot the fishing boat on the fjord with an RIB in tow. From up here, in the light of the full moon, the boat's wake spreads out like a cloth of embroidered lacework, cascading, foaming white, across the silvery water. It brings a smile to my face, though I can't hold it for long with this painful wound on my cheek, and besides I have felt increasingly gloomy since this morning. The view is certainly enchanting, but from where I stand now, I see nothing but a threat out there in the water. My feelings aren't unfounded, they are a logical response to the measurements recorded by the research buoy nearby. The data series shows that the temperatures are too high for the time of year. The thought of the consequences is dizzying: a drop in available nutrients, a decline in breeding populations. But then when I find myself fantasizing about my thesis and the contribution it will make to our understanding of the climate's impact on seabirds, I have to admit that my mood lightens a notch. Anyway, it's time to drive back to the cabin, because the captain is now steering his boat towards the peninsula and the bay.

On the drive back, I observe the reflective poles flashing past, like the days I have spent out here. Then I see the wide-open landscape, the empty space, the absence of Jo. What if conditions prove too challenging both for the birds and for him? What if neither arrives?

The captain is busy loading the crates into the RIB as I park the scooter near the cabin. I wave and call out, and he returns my greeting with two fingers to his forehead. The full moon, combined with the high pressure, has caused an extremely low tide, exposing seaweed and kelp and pebbles. He drives the RIB as close as he can, but pulls up the engine as he approaches the shallows and hauls the boat further into land with an oar. The aluminium hull scrapes against the pebbles with such a loud clanking and grating that I shudder, unaccustomed as I am now to the metallic sounds of civilization.

I come down to join him and set to work. The urgency of the task precludes any pleasantries. The boat must be moored before it glides out with the tide. I take the rope, tie it to a rusty iron ring and then immediately wade out to the boat. The cold invades my boots. I have to keep moving so my toes and feet don't freeze. I take the crates from him, barrels of water, petrol cans, and go back and forth across the shallows and up onto the shore as smoothly, as quickly, as I can. I notice a look in his eyes nonetheless, a scepticism mixed with a hint of concern. I'm still limping, despite my efforts to stride about normally, and there's the gash on my cheek. No doubt he's wondering what happened.

He swings himself out of the boat and, pulling his parka around him, takes the last box from the thwart, lifts it onto his shoulder and wades to the shore, from where I have started carrying the supplies into the shed. We work well together and after a few trips all the boxes are in place.

Coffee?

He nods, wiping his forehead with the back of his hand. I feel the moisture trickle down my spine and the cold spread across my shirt. I am sweaty but also frozen to the marrow in my hands, legs and feet, and when I point to the door with a wizened finger and invite him into the warmth, my voice cracks like glass between my rattling teeth.

Safely indoors, I stoke up the stove, boil some water for coffee and put out a little selection from the fresh supplies: bread, butter, some cheese and jam. The captain is watching me with interest, so as I walk back and forth between the kitchen and living area I try again to move easily and normally. Unfortunately I knock into the rocking chair on the way to the kitchen counter and he's instantly at my side, pointing at my foot and asking if I need help. I brush him off with a little laugh, saying that I've managed on my own this far. That's clear, he answers quickly, before asking: How did it happen? Oh, there's not much to tell, I reply with my back to him. One has to expect the occasional mishap.

Soon we're sitting side by side at the table, in a clear space between my books and PC, facing a view towards the end of the fjord and the open sea. After we've eaten I talk a bit about my work, but suddenly, in the middle of an in-depth explanation about the consequences of rising levels of carbon dioxide in the sea, he suddenly butts in to tell me that some guys he knew had set up base here for the grouse-hunting season a few years back. Oh really, I say curtly, but then with polite interest ask if the hunting round here is still good. 'Tis indeed, he answers, the catch were fine, but the challenges of this place were sommat else. But you're getting on all right, are you?

The captain looks at me with a sidelong stare. A searching, serious look. I don't know what to say. Perhaps I simply haven't considered this place in the way he's hinting at. I have research to complete, I have fled a situation, I am waiting for my lover. The captain is a respected figure in the district, responsible for transporting goods to the remotest parts of the fjord. Communication between us has largely been digital so far, and even on the trip out here he said virtually nothing. So what does he want to tell me now?

His gaze is steady, drawn only now and then to the gash in my cheek. But his mouth moves, silently opening and shutting like a fish snapping at the air on dry land, and when he is finally ready he delivers his hard-won words, slowly and emphatically.

Captain: 'Tis no place for a lonesome lass.

Me: May I must remind you that I'm here first and foremost as a researcher.

Captain: Well, things can quickly get out of hand here, even for a researcher. You'll have seen that for yerself.

Me: It really is rather cheeky of you to underestimate me like that.

Captain: I'm just trying to say that a lady oughtn't be out here alone.

Me: I'm managing. There's no need to worry.

Captain: I'll say it a little more clearly. 'Tis a long way from civilization if something were to happen. Folk have experienced that here before.

Me: Yes, it's remote and the weather is harsh. You don't need you to tell me that.

Captain: Right, but it in't the weather I'm thinking of.

I shiver, go into my alcove, fetch a shawl and pull it round my shoulders. On my return he follows me closely with his gaze, but I've already decided not to get drawn into the story he is burning to tell. I don't want to give him that power after the way he has belittled me and my fieldwork, although I have a suspicion he's thinking of the fatal fire and the tragedy that happened here the following year. I pull back my chair before sitting down, but he instantly moves closer. Listen, he says quietly. I reckon you should tell me a bit about the situation out here, how things are with you. Then he clamps a hand round my upper arm.

What is he referring to? The loneliness of life here in the cabin or to my injuries? Or to the fact that I am a woman alone in the wilderness, cut off from any sexual interaction with men? His hand – large, broad, with dark rims around the nails – feels firm and warm through my woollens. He doesn't loosen his grip and I don't pull away, almost hypnotized by the sudden warmth of another human being. I look at his fingers and think of the body that carried the boxes, a working man, ten or fifteen years older than me, white skin, thinly distributed, greying hairs on his chest and back, a roll of fat around his midriff, powerful thigh muscles and sinewy arms. I imagine him naked, his cock shrunken, a miserable, wrinkly rag over heavy testicles, but then a vigorous erection, firm and fleshy, with a strutting red head, right here, here in the middle of the cabin floor. I see him grabbing his cock, stroking my lips with a rough thumb, telling me to open my mouth, lick his balls, suck him dry, there on the chair, in the fine light from the window.

I push the images and his hand away, determinedly, leaving no room for misunderstanding. You can forget that, I say, getting up to clear the table. He looks at me wearily, takes a slurp of his coffee, wipes his mouth. I reckon the lady misunderstands, he says, putting his cup down on the table.

Again I wonder if I've lost the ability to interpret human signals in these last weeks. Surely he was trying to make a move? I walk over to the kitchen, rattle the kettle deliberately loudly on the cooker, and think how I should have asked him if I could weigh and measure his cock first. As a researcher I'd want to assure myself that it was the real thing between his legs. Or ought I to apologize, in case he's in the right? Whatever, I must tread more carefully, as I wouldn't want my research to run aground for lack of provisions. So I bustle about, my every gesture expressing that it's time for him to get himself together and leave. In anticipation of our parting, I put the cutlery and plates in the washing-up bowl and squeeze out a few drops of washing-up liquid, but as I'm about to pour in the freshly boiled water, he surprises me by loosening his vocal cords. Words gush from him, as though, like the water, he has reached boiling point.

Captain: Listen, I don't want to say this, but your ex contacted me. He asked me to keep him informed of the situation out here. He wants to be sure that everything's OK with you out here alone.

Captain: It might seem kindly enough on the part of an ex, but he was so insistent that I ain't too sure if I should tell him the truth. These here supplies are clearly calculated for two. Where your companion might be is not my business, but you're clearly not as alone as he thinks.

Captain: So I were wondering, should I tell your ex? Would he find it reassuring, or is it sommat he ought not to know?

I turn to the captain, hands behind my back, and grasp the edge of the countertop, hold myself steady, dizzy, afraid to break down in front of him, right here on the floor. S knows about my project, of course, and where I am, but being so far from civilization, beyond his control, I assumed I was safe. Safe – as long as he thought I was alone.

Me: You can tell him whatever you want. But I eat for two out here. I use a lot of energy in a working day.

Captain: Yes, I can understand that. But shaving foam and razors aren't exactly something a lady requires...

Me: You've got a cheek! My hair growth is of no concern to you.

We stand at opposite ends of the cabin, the captain's gaze glinting like razor-sharp steel. I've offended him, that's clear, and now he seeks retribution in crude patriarchal style. Or is this man, on the contrary, trying to convey information so alarming that I immediately interpret it as an attack?

The captain picks up his parka, shoves his arms in, lifts it over his back and twists his body into place in his voluminous jacket. He makes to leave, then pauses expectantly at the front door, clearly in the hope that I might admit to something or other. But I've nothing to add to what has already been said, so he ends the conversation himself as he goes to turn the door handle.

Captain: I really don't know which of you worries me most – you or your ex. Anyway. This place has a bad reputation. I think I ought to check on things here soonish – in a couple of weeks. Reckon that's what's best for you.

29

Pressure, strength, heat, speed, measured in hectopascals, metres per second, percentages and degrees Celsius, represent a clear language I'm used to interpreting. I even see something as ungraspable and elusive as a sudden infatuation as the result of a measurable, atmospheric disturbance. A solar wind, for example, was hurled to earth at the exact moment Jo turned to me for the first time. A stream of charged particles the eye cannot see, which I nonetheless caught a glint of and which I have therefore described again and again with that well-worn phrase: The look in his eyes, that's what I fell for.

Everything can be explained rationally. Or so I thought, until now.

The tracks around the cabin, the prints in the snow from foxes and mice and hares, are clear and to be expected in a place like this. But I notice something else. Something more. Here. In the bay. And maybe inside the cabin too. It is possible that the captain's visit has activated my senses and caused me to see this place, my experiences here, from a more obscure angle. But I have no idea what it is, this thing I'm detecting, and thus I have no solid data to confirm its existence. Only a certain unease. Recurring physiological fluctuations that grow in frequency as they rise from my stomach to my chest. An unease that, if it were plotted on a graph, would show a marked and rapid escalation in both scope and intensity.

Presumably this state of high alert accounts for my extreme reactions. I come into the cabin one evening carrying an armful of logs. The room is barely lit by the wall lamps, with a trembling orange reflection in the night-black window. I shut the front door, stamp the snow off onto the mat and go over to the stove. In the dark, my gaze is involuntarily drawn to the flicker of light. I suddenly freeze, instinctively pulling my arms closer to myself, until I feel the stiff bark of the logs cutting into my wrists. Standing there, outside the window, is Borghild, clear as can be. Her face is pale, her eyes, hidden in two deep hollows, stare right at me, while her hands, as skinny as claws, clutch a bundle, the little child, which she holds close to her. In my arms, I feel the weight of the wood and press the logs even harder against my chest to suppress the scream that rises from my throat, escapes my lips, dry and soundless at first, before it suddenly bursts out, with uneasy fluctuations, from deep within me. I scream as I hear the logs crash into the stove in time with Borghild as she lets go of her child, scream as I see the bundle disappear, vanish from the window, scream at the face out there, ravaged by fear and despair.

I can barely breathe. Every muscle seems bathed in lactic acid. My arms and my legs are numb, devoid of sensation as I stagger towards the kitchen counter. I fill a glass with water, lift it to my mouth, feel the cool, clear liquid spread, seep into my brain, washing away the dream-like haze, allowing myself to emerge from this abyss of fantasies. I realize almost immediately, of course, that it was my own reflection I saw in the window. But I am nonetheless shaken. Shaken by the rupture of my own perception, by my mind, by my ability to summon up an image, so clear, so utterly visual, not just as a thought but as a presence, outside myself, completely lifelike and real.

30

Perhaps I'm a bit like the nature out here. Worn down to bare rock by the cold, windy winters and sudden, short summers. The drifts of ice and frost hide cracks and wounds, but as the sun takes hold and the ice melts, tiny shoots emerge defiantly, surprisingly strong, with petals of lilac, yellow or red. I see myself in this image. I can be shaken, I can be bent, I can be crushed, but like a vigorous stem I will always grow back, reaching out towards clarity and light. So when, at about five this morning, I was confronted again with something vague and intangible, I forced myself to observe the event, albeit using an unscientific approach.

I was woken by a child crying. I don't like to think it, or admit it, not one bit. I certainly don't want to enter the statistics of lonely researchers who get lost in their own psyche. Yet the sound was undeniable, as real as my fingers and toes, and instead of refusing to relate to my senses, instead of dismissing it all as a figment of my imagination, I tried to welcome the event with a so-called open mind.

A faint hiccuping, the type that follows a lengthy sob, was what I heard. Sad and inconsolable, interspersed with the occasional sniff. I lay for a long time just listening, and although I was not directly fearful, my sympathetic nervous system reacted instantly, initiating a series of adrenalin-fuelled processes. My heart beat fast and hard, my muscles tensed, my breathing grew heavier, but some minutes later I managed to sit up in bed and listen more keenly. First, I heard the wind, the full spectrum of rattling and cracking and grinding sounds from the loose roofing felt, then the sighing through the cracks and gaps in the walls, the whispering through the cabin, from the sleeping alcove to the kitchen and living area, the creaking of the timber frame, the crackling in the stove. I tuned in to the minutest trickle of water or hint of a murmur, separating one sound from another, identifying them. And yes, the generator was switched off for the night.

Then I left my bed to seek the source of the cry. I stood on the icy floor in my alcove, listened to the walls, the ceiling, and lay on the floor with my ear against the boards. I went out into the living area, repeated the procedure, investigating every nook and cranny, but the crying did not grow or diminish in volume. It seemed to come from everywhere, as though I was both its goal and its centre.

As I stood there listening, it struck me that something about its tone might resemble Lina's cry, though I have never heard her sobbing like that, so utterly desolate and alone. But once I had made this connection, I heard only her. It was Lina, my little girl, who was crying. My curiosity dissolved with a bang and there in that room I saw one thing only: Lina. Her face, the clear gaze that absorbs her surroundings with such trusting wonder. Lina, who doesn't grasp what's happening and reaches out for closeness and reassurance. That thought, that image, was unbearable. I covered my ears with my hands, closed my eyes, but when I felt the tears running, I took a fold in my skin and pinched it until my nails entered my flesh, until the physical pain was all I registered. I gasped with an open mouth, a short, loud intake of breath, which seemed to expand and fill the room. In that instant it felt as though the sobbing itself registered my presence. There was a pause, a vibrating moment, before it picked up and started again, but fainter this time, before it ebbed into a soft whistling sound, and then all I could hear was the whining of the wind.

I stood for a while listening to the familiar sounds, noting how rational and absolutely measurable each was, as I stroked my hands over my face, down my neck and chest, as though to rid myself of the last remnants of my discomfort. I stroked and stroked, until I was sure and certain of one thing: it was the echo of my own consciousness I had heard. I had allowed my own worries to play themselves out. For myself and myself alone.

31

It cannot be avoided any longer. I must confront myself, answer the questions I still haven't asked. How can I be certain that S gives Lina the care she needs?

I still don't understand it, this capacity S has to be so attentive. It stands out as an anomaly among the traits that dominate his personality. The man who seems so unapproachable and reticent, who can come across with an intensity that borders on the tactless, can also be attractive if you interpret the intensity as an expression of devotion. Perhaps it was this gushing attention that I fell in love with, because it made me feel strong and important. But when this same quality morphed into a form of control, a demand for an almost spliced-together *we*, it created nothing but emptiness in me.

It's not hard to remember the feeling of being stuck, unable to escape, of being a fly in the spider's web, living food for someone who, under the guise of having needs, expects to possess you more than you do yourself. Yet it is in this very gesture of encircling me, of imposing such intimacy and then perhaps accusing me afterwards of not being close or present enough, this gesture of concentrated interest, of intense attention, that I think I see him as being good for Lina. And Lina's childish affection, her mere presence, makes him feel contented enough to let me go bit by bit. More precisely, by handing Lina over to S I am stabilizing him and saving myself.

So far, so good. But caring comes from somewhere else entirely. For caring is not necessarily caring as it is in the seabirds, where both parents instinctively and naturally share the tasks. No, in human beings, caring is as much a means, a method, and for you particularly, S, caring is an exercise of power, and Lina herself is the trophy. For with every nappy you change in public, in front of the family, your friends, with every spoon you put in her mouth, every comforting word you utter, you demonstrate your exemplary commitment, and also what a useless, perfidious mother I am. But I want to say this, S, compared to another father, my lover, your rival, the care you offer is as bad as you perceive mine to be. And the comparison, the account sheet, runs like this:

Jo gives care. You dispense caring.

Jo acts intuitively. You do nothing but what you have understood and learned.

Jo sets himself aside whenever it's needed. You do what is expected, neither more nor less.

Jo's caring is rooted in a natural empathy, a sensitivity that cannot be measured or weighed. Yours, on the contrary, follows set standards.

And not least, for Jo caring is something natural, to be taken for granted, while you primarily perform for the acknowledgement you will receive.

So don't come here and tell me what caring is. That you, S, are a self-sacrificing, selfless father. It is only your own reflection you care for, as you swagger around with Lina on your arm.

So say I. I who cannot even think of her, of her arms, her fingers, the chubbiness, the roundness, the softness, the laughter, so trusting that my chest and shoulders tremble. I who cannot think of the kisses, the light in her eyes, Lina at the dinner table, at play, in bed, at home with me, in my apartment. I who scarcely dare acknowledge my longing, or grief at her absence. I who drown out the memories, who blot out these images with fantasies, daydreams, a stranger, Niels.

32

One morning I stand in the middle of the cabin with the hunting rifle in my hands. It is cold, but the sky is clear and the visibility good. Overnight the wind has dropped considerably so that it moves lightly, almost tenderly, across the bay, across the roof of the cabin. A wind speed of roughly two metres per second, I estimate, before moving on to guess the speed of a shot from this rifle, of a projectile as it exits the muzzle: 800 metres per second is not unthinkable. It is a traditional hunting rifle and you have to pull the trigger for each shot, but by way of compensation this type of gun is more accurate than, for example, a semi-automatic weapon. This is the sort of thing I know from my time in the hunting team.

In the middle of the day, with the sun like an eye glinting just above the horizon, I drive to the end of the isthmus, where the landscape flattens out with fjords on either side. The rifle hangs on a strap over my shoulder, the ammunition is stowed under my seat. In the trailer, five empty tin cans and five reflective poles rattle against the petrol can and shovels that I take on every trip.

I park near a sparse patch of willow that pokes up from the windblown snow and here I set up the five reflective poles, placing the tin cans on top with a distance of about twenty metres between each. I drive back and forth to inspect them and, after straightening one or two, they stand like a row of other-worldly knights in helmets with open visors. Satisfied, I drive on in a southerly direction, and in a gentle dip in the terrain, with a low sun behind me, I turn off the engine to consider my attack on this line-up of targets. White-crested waves roll in across the fjords on both sides, and when I follow the flight of two black-backed gulls over the isthmus, I discover that the sky in the north is darkened with a stormy front. I touch the dressing on my cheek, feel the pressure of the inflammation and all at once the targets ahead of me seem to stand ready for battle, a fierce glint in the metal.

I get back on the scooter and, with my head just above the steering bar and my knees around the tank, I press the start button. The acceleration is resolute and I speed across the blue-white slopes, straight towards the first tin can. Around thirty metres away I stop and, with the engine idling, get into position, one foot on the brake and the other on the seat. I take out the rifle, set the butt against my shoulder and the barrel over the scooter's windscreen, then aim at my target. My index finger presses on the trigger, cold but firm. I breathe in three times and fire the first shot, before quickly reloading and shooting again. The recoil is powerful and as I press the accelerator and drive on to the next tin I can feel a tingling in my chest and ringing in my ears, as if electrically charged particles were whizzing back and forth between my alveoli and eardrums. I repeat the procedure – rise, shoot, reload and shoot again, decisive, focused – ten times in all. But midway, after the fifth shot, as I fill the chamber with ammunition, I suddenly become aware of my surroundings. Or my surroundings become aware of me.

I hear the scooter roar like a raging beast with the friction against the hard snow and ice crusts. I hear the cracking and booming sounds, which without echo or reverberation shatter the silence of this wide-open space like a protracted explosion. Then I hear the sound of metal being pierced and shattered, the hollow clatter of tin cans as they somersault across the snow-packed ground, the mutilation of a fundamental peace. All the while, as unrest proliferates, wave after wave, as the sun-eye sinks, darkness flares up, the sooty clouds hastily shroud the waning moon until my own shadow disappears, and the lights on my scooter cut into the landscape like swords. I see it, I hear it, the disturbance I am inflicting, and as I collect the tin cans, one from the last pole, four spread around on the slopes, I sense a wary disquiet, in the natural world as much as in myself, about my desire to strike out, and my own precision.

33

I look over my shoulder several times on my way back, suddenly and without thought. I don't know why or what I'm looking for exactly, I just do it, as though my body and will were divided. My mind is drawn involuntarily towards the mapping of seabirds, in particular the new technology that can provide detailed information about their behaviour and movements throughout the entire year. I think of digital surveillance cameras placed in the research field during nesting which automatically film a section of the colony at given times of the day. I think of satellite transmitters, no more than four or five grams in weight, that can be mounted on the birds' bodies like rucksacks, tracking their position continuously. I think of light data loggers that are also used to map migratory routes and wintering grounds, with which the birds' positions can be calculated from the length of the days and intensity of light. And GPS loggers that also store data that makes it possible to map the birds' migration over the sea and transponders that are inserted under the skin and give automatic readings of the birds' movements. I think of all these things as I speed away with my thumb firmly on the accelerator, about all the activities that can be so closely observed while an unsuspecting subject gets on with its life. Or might a kittiwake sense, just as I do, a disturbing presence?

I accelerate as I approach the bay. I have left the part of the isthmus that is sheltered by the cliffs and here, where the landscape opens out towards the fjord and sea, I feel a surprising resistance from the wind that rolls in from the north. The shift in the weather is unexpected and may be due to a polar low pressure, not impossible judging by the decisive rise in wind strength. I follow the trail as best I can in the scooter's wavering lights, but the wind sweeps over the tracks like an invisible hand erasing the line that cuts across the landscape and down towards the fjord. Now and then I glimpse the glow of the cabin's outside lamp, which bobs into view as though from a distressed ship lost in high waves, as massive and seething as the turbulent waters near the headland beyond. I accelerate to outrun the wind, but visibility is dropping fast and soon these glimpses of light are all I have to navigate by. But I'm reasonably sure about the way now, and when I'm nearly there I increase my speed a little more, hungry and tired and ready for the warmth of the stove. Between two small mounds I come to a sudden standstill, exactly where the snow is at its loosest and deepest, an area that, had the conditions been different, I'd have been wary of and avoided. I hit the accelerator in an attempt to get my scooter out of the dip. The engine screeches, the belt spins, snow sprays into the air, but the scooter only digs itself in deeper, until the rear, together with the trailer, is buried in a shallow V. Shit. Fuck. The swear words continue to pour out of me as I slide down from my seat and haul my feet step by step through the snow, drag myself to the trailer to get my shovel. The wind tugs and tears at the plastic sheeting that I need to lift momentarily. And when I straighten up again, I'm nearly blown over. I try to figure out where I am. I glimpse the cabin just a stone's throw away and, as I realize my exact location, it dawns on me that I'm stuck in one of the furrows that once marked the foundations of a house. For a moment I stand there in immobilized bewilderment, but when a sharp pain grabs at my ankle, like an echo of my fall down the slope, I feel an urgent desire to get away. I unhitch the trailer, drag it to the side and, with my back to the fjord and the wind, launch myself at the mounds of snow around the scooter. Spadeful after spadeful is thrown and scraped aside, but large quantities swirl up into the air to form a dense blizzard. With that my optimism fades. I've got to face it: the disturbed snow simply resettles in heaps that cover any area as fast as I clear it. Besides, digging is not what's needed here, but firm and steady ground that offers good grip. I hurl the shovel into the snow. I have neither the energy nor the time for such a task, not in this wind at least; the best thing is to abandon the scooter and go by foot. I fetch the rifle, sling it over my shoulder and, with the rest of the ammunition in my pocket, head for the cabin. I glance back only once. It is an arresting sight. The scooter's skis seem to reach out to me from where they are protruding over the edge, and the headlights stare into the blizzard with an extinguished, helpless gaze, as though this great and powerful machine is giving up hope.

There should be at least two people on fieldwork: a researcher and an assistant, who work side by side. That's how it ought to have been and that is how it will be. But as I struggle on in the wind, it's not without a touch of anxiety. Although, measured against the gusts that come at me like bullets, my despondency is like a pinprick. I have to lean right into the wind, fight for every inch of progress. But my endurance is greater than the opposition, there is nothing to fear. Still, it can't be ignored that nature is superior. If it comes to a protracted battle, nature will win. It will let me think I have the upper hand, but then suddenly strike out from an unexpected angle. If it doesn't finish me off right away, it will annihilate me so slowly that I barely notice. It has been this way since the dawn of time.

Nonetheless, humans beat nature increasingly often. Here, at the bird cliff, the great auk is a fearful example. Its tasty meat and soft, downy feathers, combined with a helpless gait and the inability to fly, made the poor bird attractive game. This species was systematically hunted to extinction. It is claimed that the last individual was shot in eastern Norway in 1840. Now it's as though I am in the middle of a firing line myself, with the loud thunder of the waves on one side and a persistent screeching across the bay on the other, and the resistance that increases with each step I take towards the cabin. The wind is tugging at my scooter suit. I am being buffeted so hard that I am forced to stoop, with my hands in front of my face, and when the gusts are at their strongest I have to lie flat so as not to be flung into the air. I battle on, groping my way forwards with a growing unease, a disturbing feeling of being hunted down by a manifestation of wrath. And the more I think about it, the more clearly the storm takes the form of a conscious, living being. I can feel it, see its damaged soul, filled with a pain and despair so great that it wants to tear both me and the bay into shreds. *Olaf*, I think to myself in a confused moment, feeling the breath catch in my windpipe: is this where his rage has deposited itself, forever bound to the wind and the forces of nature?

A vulnerability assessment, that's what this place and I need, I think as the entrance to the cabin comes into view. A calculation of the probability that we will weaken or die out within a specified time frame. The simulations being based on the understanding that we will experience the same variation in environmental conditions in the future as we have experienced in a given period, the final classification of vulnerability being made according to the red-list categories. The question is where on the list we find ourselves, and with that thought I dive through my front door. On the floor, shivering and frostbitten, with the storm whipping around the room, I see it clearly. During these last few weeks, my status has changed from vulnerable to critically endangered.

34

His fist slams into the door frame so hard that he clutches the meaty back of his hand with a grimace. Her instinct is to get up and take his fist in hers, to feel the weight of it, while in the light of the cod liver oil lamp she studies the rough, dry skin, the dark wrinkles and cracked fingertips, before opening his hand out and placing it full-length over her face, pressing her nose and mouth into the hollow of his palm, and there, where the skin is softest, taking in his smell, gently licking in the taste of earth, salt and metal, before she presses her lips to it and kisses him softly. But how can she do that when he is turned from her with stooped shoulders, because she has said or done something again that caused such a strong reaction in him that he is hammering and punching walls and timbers?

They've been living in the new house for a couple of months now, but it's still far from complete. There's a rickety ladder where there should be stairs to the attic, and until these are finished they sleep on the kitchen floor, while the girls have their room further in. The door which should divide the two rooms leans on a half-finished wall.

The windows lack mouldings and the benches and kitchen cupboards are just nailed together, an emergency solution until he has time to make better ones, like the ones they had before.

She is careful not to complain, he has enough to do, but it's impossible not to notice that the housebuilding has been reduced to a chore. Where their previous house was built with precision, strong and solid from corner to corner, the new one has been hastily assembled, an indifferent copy. But that's not all. He treats her in the same way, perfunctorily, as though she's a bother. In the evening, lying next to the stove, on thin mattresses of jute sacks and straw, Olaf glances over at her before he turns his back. If she puts a hand on his shoulder, he shakes her off and whispers in a low, urgent tone that the children can hear them. During the day he goes fishing and hunting or tends the sheep. He avoids her just as he avoids the house. But where he is distant and brooding, she appears light and contented. And the darker he gets, the happier and more open she is. She can catch herself laughing when she should meet him with seriousness, smiling when she should offer him sympathy, and when she should move carefully, show sensitivity and tact, she can blurt out whatever is on her mind. It'll be nice, she might say, when the girls move up to the attic. Or, this draught makes my feet and hands awfully stiff at the spinning wheel, there'll be neither warmth nor clothes for you if this continues, my dear husband. Or she might blurt out humorously: Oh me, oh my! I never did see such woeful misery!

They are two opposite poles that magnify the difference between them, and as the contrast grows more obvious, they each push the other further into their separate lonely path. A dense darkness and an overwhelming light, that is what they have become, as they sit at either end of the plank table with the children in the grey zone between them. He absorbed in his bowl of soup, she chatting lightly with their daughters about chores and duties. As with his heaviness and her lightness, the open chasm between them is something she ignores, while he seems to see it everywhere, in the bottom of his soup bowl as much as in her eyes.

At night he is restless, turning this way and that in bed before finally getting up with a groan. She often wakes, but pretends to be asleep still, and squinting through a gap in her covers she follows his movements around the room. Sometimes she sees him run his fingers over the axe marks in the log walls, or she hears him swallow hard, pottering about and turning over little things that have been left out, a spoon, stones and shells the children have brought in, or sitting on the bench to leaf through the Bible. She usually falls asleep to the words he recites in a devout whisper, and the sigh on the air as the crisp pages are carefully turned, interspersed now and then with a delicate crackling as he leafs quickly on. On this particular night, however, she stays awake. A summer breeze, heavy with the fragrance of the seashore and freshly cut grass, streams through the window that stands ajar. The dawn light plays on the windowpane, so that from where she lies on the floor, his head and torso seem encircled by a radiant light, as though he were filled with the word of God. Peace at last, she thinks, wanting to get up and embrace him, and perhaps ask forgiveness. This happiness of hers is hard-won and feigned. If she were to hold on to the tragedy and sorrow, as he has done, an evil darkness would spread and take over their home entirely. No, she has carried her hope like a fragile flame through a winter, spring and summer, held it close, close to her breast, guarded it as something sacred for herself and them all. She continues to do just that as she rises, steps softly across the floor, sits beside him, and in the light from the window and with a hand on his arm, she asks in a faint whisper if he can show her forbearance.

He pulls his arm away. You take it too lightly, he says, casting a sidelong glance at her hand, which lies like a useless, withered extremity between them. I don't understand it, he continues. Our lives will be built out of a sea of ashes and you expect everything to be as it was before? But it won't. Nothing will be as it was. Our son is dead. Our house burned down. And what I can't stand, can't bear, is that laughter of yours, that voice which rings so bright and so loud that my head feels it will burst. I curse it, do you know that? I curse the way you take everything so lightly, that's the real tragedy: the way you go around smiling as though nothing had happened. I curse it, I curse you and all of your kind, and will until the end of my days. Do you understand?

35

Just weeks before coming out here, one weekend in December when Lina was staying with me, Jo invited us to his home for dinner and to stay the night with him and Maria. We were going to celebrate the fact that all the formalities and practicalities were in place for my fieldwork. It was the last night he and I would spend together before my departure.

I felt I was lifted out of the battle that S and I had been locked in. The new year ahead seemed bathed in light. Just as the sun would rise, my research and my relationship with Jo would develop and fall into place. I felt an airy lightness, an endless freedom, as though I had been lifted up, far above every conceivable hindrance. S could continue to rant and rave. I was getting away.

How happy I was that afternoon. Jo and Maria had decorated the tables and sideboards with Christmas elves and angels made out of kitchen rolls and shiny paper. Red and green garlands hung from the ceiling between strings of glittering fairy lights and on a little table in front of the living-room window was a gingerbread house they had made, buckling under the weight of icing and boiled sweets and a sprinkling of brightly coloured chocolate drops. Candles were lit and little bowls of fruit and sweets put out, and in the background cheerful Christmas music filled the rooms.

Feeling at home, I went around pointing out little details to Lina, laughed and joked with Maria, and while Jo fried some mince and cut up the accompaniments for tacos, I went between him and the living room, observed him, studied his body and posture, his buttocks and shoulders, the nape of his neck where his hair always comes to a point, his gestures as he worked, the muscles and sinews in his arms and hands, the interplay of strength and sensitivity, firmness and lightness, in his fingertips around a tomato, in the slice of the knife.

Lina clung to me, a finger in her mouth as she gazed about her, wide-eyed. She had met Jo several times, and Maria too, although clearly not often enough for her to dare to let go of me. Or was she just overwhelmed by all the Christmas frippery, the music and the atmosphere, and even by my behaviour, that I was so openly and unrestrainedly merry? It didn't occur to me at the time, but I see it now. This was hardly consistent with our everyday lives, in which she was dragged between S and myself. And whenever she stayed with me, I was probably more concerned with the preparations for my fieldwork than with folding shiny paper or baking gingerbread.

Over the course of the evening she began to relax, not least because of Maria, who involved her in a game in which she was the baby and Maria the mother. Jo and I got a moment's breathing space on the sofa, and we drank coffee and ate the leftovers of dessert as we watched the game unfold. Maria instructed her to lie on the floor with her head on a cushion, and as she fussed about her with blankets and covers, she told her to cry. You must cry, said Maria encouragingly, with no response from Lina. You must cry, *all* babies cry, she continued impatiently. But Lina did not make a sound, she just lay there, clutching the edge of the coverlet, her eyes fixed on me.

I wasn't really taking much notice. My attention was directed towards Jo. I wanted to discuss the trip to the bird cliff, the challenges around the collection of data, everything the two of us could expect in the months we were away. We had discussed the subject countless times, of course, but tonight it felt doubly important that he say something solid and concrete and give me the reassurances I needed. He nodded at what I said, contributing the odd *absolutely* and *of course*, and with a little smile repeated again that we'd better hope for large atmospheric pressure variations in the North Atlantic Oscillation this year. But that was about it, because *his* attention was directed towards the children. Lina seems insecure, he said, interrupting me in my preamble about a similar project we had already discussed, but whose significance I suddenly felt the need to point out. She clings to you, he went on undeterred, have you noticed? I took a second to gather my thoughts, readied myself to interject with some further edifying comment, straightened up, took a deep breath, but restrained myself with a feeling of being misunderstood.

Was I distant? Was Lina unsure of me? Of me! When we were together we barely knew where she started and I stopped: we were *one* stream, *one* movement, *one* direction. I saw her and did not see her. There was insufficient distance between us, just as between myself and my reflection. So how could I possibly accept what Jo had pointed out – her clinging to me – as an indication of the opposite? No. It was the very essence of a symbiosis he had glimpsed. Of being so tightly bonded, so utterly saturated in each other's senses and feelings, that neither can see the other beyond an *us*.

I wanted to say something like that. But instead I said: She's so used to having me to herself. This evening I need time for you and time for her, and I'm sharing it out as best I can.

Afterwards, in the kitchen, I grabbed him as he stood loading the dishwasher and nuzzled into his neck with my mouth and nose. I recognized the surprising sense of calm he gave me. Just his smell, the closeness to his skin, his hair, could stabilize any mental unrest.

When the last cartoon was over, we each carried our child up to the bathroom. Jo filled the tub and poured in a generous splash of bubble bath, and while I brushed the girls' teeth, he prepared the bed in Maria's room. They were going to sleep head to toe, which was completely new and strange for Lina. To prepare her, I described how much fun it would be to have Maria's toes tickling her. Lina giggled as, holding her under her arms, I let her slender body slip slowly through the foam blanket and down into the water, at the opposite end to Maria, who was already blowing bubbles into the air. That's how you two are going to sleep, I said, crouching down beside the tub, smoothing out and pushing away the fluffy surface as it rose and swelled. I turned off the tap and pushed the bubbles aside again, but they still kept mounting up, and when a thick carpet of bubbles gathered under Lina's chin she began to cry.

She continued like this for the rest of the evening. Everything I did was wrong. Towelling her dry, brushing her hair, putting her pyjamas on. And when I carried her into the room where she was going to sleep, she let go of me and flung herself backwards with an ear-splitting howl. Maria sat in the bed with a crestfallen and weary expression. You're not meant to cry now, she said pointedly to Lina, not when we're meant to be going to sleep. I sat on the edge of the bed, lifted the duvet and patted the pillow, sang and hummed all her favourite songs, chatted about trivial and familiar things, but Lina twisted and turned, sweaty and blotchy from the screaming that only got worse. In an attempt to distract her, Jo came back in to say goodnight again. Maria put an arm around her father's neck and clung to him, then with a hand cupped to his ear she whispered something, to which he gently but firmly shook his head. Her lower lip trembled, a quiver that spread to her chin, and when she could no longer control herself, she took a sharp intake of breath and began to cry too.

We took their mattress into Jo's room and there, on the floor at the end of the bed where we lay, the two girls slept, exhausted and tear-stained.

The street lamp outside cast a dull yellow glow through the curtains. Jo was lying on his side, with his back to the faint light, so that from my position his facial features were blotted out, lost in darkness, while the contours of his head, neck and shoulders were sharp and clear. I reached out a hand, fumbling through empty space until I felt his hand take mine, squeeze it and hold it to his chest. I drew closer, put my lips against the hollow of his neck and gently stroked his stomach, then heard him whisper into my hair that he didn't want to make love now, with the children right there.

I lay on my back. Minutes turned into a quarter of an hour, then half an hour. It was impossible to sleep. I burned like the street lamp, aware of the light on his skin, glinting smooth over tendons and muscles. I burned to make our contract manifest, tongue against tongue, to move on top of him, to press myself down until his sex stood rigid in mine, and there leave an unbreakable seal stamped with a last indelible memory.

I burned, crackled like a light arc in an electrical flash-over, until I heard him whisper again in a hoarse voice from the dark:

It beats me how you can find it so easy to leave Lina for so long.

And after a short pause: Don't get me wrong. I know your work's important to you and that you need to get away from S for a while, but I find this decision of yours so problematic that I don't even know what I think about you any more.

36

14 February, eleven o'clock. Observations at the cabin. Temperature: minus one point two degrees Celsius. Wind: fresh breeze from the south, ten point three metres per second. Cloud cover: six eighths. Stratocumulus.

I stand at the front door looking out over the bay with my sheepskin hat in my hands, absently rubbing the fur between my fingers, and ascertain that the weather has, like my existence here, stabilized once again. I straighten up and draw breath, feel the icy draught fill my lungs, spreading from the alveoli and into my bloodstream with fresh and invigorating oxygen. I breathe in and out so hard that the carbon dioxide streams like a mini whirlwind from my mouth and my body quivers with energy and power. I laugh aloud, a mocking laughter directed at the surrounding landscape. Here I am again! Alive and kicking! Damned if I'll let myself be broken, either by bad weather or by some measly accident!

Feeling uplifted, snowshoes strapped on, tools in my inside pocket and two planks of wood under my arm, I set out on the short walk to the stranded scooter. Across the bay the snow reflects the lilac light of the sky. In places along the shoreline the slush and grainy ice have gathered into little towers that stand like neatly shaped markers between the bottles, plastic fish crates and clumps of fishing net that have been swept in during the recent storms. As I kick and drag the rubbish further up the beach, with plans for a clean-up later, I become aware of everything this place and I have to contend with. I stop and draw four hearts in the snow, one for Lina, one for Jo, one for the bird cliff and one for the sea, and with these four in mind I trudge across the last metres to my scooter.

The skis are still poking up from the foundation wall, while the back of the machine is buried under fresh drifts of thick snow. After a speedy assessment, I get started. It's hot work digging in a scooter suit, and it's difficult to move in such a big, bulky garment, but soon enough I have moved all the snow that lay on either side of the scooter, and most of the loose snow has been cleared from in front, behind and under the scooter.

Again I am struck by how beautiful and peaceful it is out here on a bright day like this. It's impossible to evoke the sinister feelings I've had lately. I think of how, on this very spot, within this rectangular space, Borghild and Olaf Berthelsen once stood, walked in and out, slept, prepared food and ate. In this spot, thoughts and words were exchanged, tears shed and both anger and laughter given expression. Life began, life was lived and then one day it came to an end, but nothing remains, there's nothing to be seen or sensed, apart from a furrow in the ground and the remains of this wall.

I turn my focus to the last part of my task. Unroll my toolkit, crouch down on the ground, prop up the springs and check that the belt is not frozen to the chassis, before grabbing one of the skis and dragging the scooter as far as I can to the side and lifting the back out of the tracks a fraction. Then I press planks down into the snow under the belt, to make the ground firmer and give the studs something to grip. With that it's ready to go. Pleased with myself, I tuck a few icy hairs under my hat. Now all I need to do is steer the scooter gently up and out of the trench. I mount it and, with my thumb lightly on the accelerator, release the power. The scooter jerks into action: the belt spins at first, but I quickly shift my weight back, release the accelerator a little and a moment later it has enough grip almost to glide over the bump.

Sweating and with a thumping heart, I throw my arms in the air and give a cry of triumph that vibrates like a falling axe across the bay: I am invincible! I can do anything!

I could of course have made more of my exhaustion here, described my aching back and arms, and how, in an effort to offset the pain in my ankle, I used muscles that don't like that kind of static work, and therefore responded by tensing up until I got cramp in my leg. I could have mentioned the freezing temperatures, the icy cold like a drill through my nails, the failure of my fine motor skills, turning my fingers into ten blunt, uncooperative helpers, and the wind. I could have mentioned the wind again, the loose snow that swirled up and settled like a sugar coating over each shovelful, that whipped my face, simultaneously sweaty and freezing, and yes, I could have mentioned my skin afterwards, the warmth indoors that made my blood vessels expand and my pores open up, the inflammation, the entire surface of my skin tight to bursting, the puffy face, purple like a drunkard.

But why would I, when I have triumphed against these adversities so overwhelmingly?

37

Sweets, red, yellow and green, slip to and fro between my tongue and palate, sour and so fiercely sweet that I have to crush a piece between my teeth, suck on the juice of the fragments until the saliva seeps out and fills my mouth. These are Jo's favourite sweets, so I ordered several bags for him, but since opening one I have on several occasions filled my mouth with as many as seven at a time. The bags are dwindling and I can see it myself, the psychological dimension: Jo's absence, the void these sweets fill, that it's somehow *him* I have roaming in my mouth, it's him I am sucking on, greedily, until the saliva runs. Not that I'm belittling the effects of these sweets on my neurobiological processes. The taste, the smell and the sight associated with the desired object release a rush of dopamine, the reward being a feeling of satisfaction and happiness. And I might add, more personally, of sunshine in every single nerve cell.

I stuffed a handful into my mouth on my drive out to the bird cliff and it's the remains that I'm now crunching between my teeth as I park the scooter near the boulder, put on my snowshoes and trudge over to the precipitation gauge and weather station. The vibrant flavours sweeten my mood, my sense of control, my conviction that my data is about to bridge the gap between theory and reality. Although an increasing number of studies show a connection between the climate and the status of seabirds, there have been, as far as I know, only ten or so articles published in international journals which document the climate's effects on North Atlantic seabirds. So the possibility of getting a scientific article about my fieldwork into print is not just likely but highly probable.

The weather mast is as I left it, bolt upright in the snow. Ice has gathered on a few of the sensors, but it won't have affected more than two days' measurements. I suck at the last tiny shard and imagine the dissolving colours. If I opened my mouth, the cavity would probably glow as intensely as the sky above, in an explosion of reds and pinks mixed with shades of yellow, in which my gullet and the masts, my spittle and the sea would be indistinguishable. I swallow the last remains, and as I carry out my usual tasks – taking pictures and downloading the data from the last two days – the wind putters as always with the sensors and makes the guy wires tremble gently.

On the trip back, uplifted by renewed belief in my stay out here, I think how lucky I've been despite everything. There are some terribly steep slopes, for example, on the journey down from the plateau to the bay, and on a day with heavy snow and poor visibility I could easily have driven off the trail, with disastrous consequences. Or I could have got stuck on the plateau in a whiteout, where the cloudy sky and snow-covered landscape merge, and the horizon and any shadows or distinguishing features become so blurred that you stand in endless white space. Without any reference points or anything on which to fix your gaze, it is impossible to see, impossible to walk and even more impossible to drive. Combined with the cold and relentless wind out here, I'd have frozen in a few hours during such a weather event. Thank God for my good fortune, I think to myself, for colours and nuances and differences, without which I am lost. And then I smile faintly at the thought that Jo, in the form of colourful sweets, is waiting for me in the cabin.

38

I am floating on a feeling of sovereignty, of invincibility, and back in the cabin it strikes me how highly I now value the robust and simple life in here. The rocking chairs, the rough plank table on its two trestles. It's as though they welcome me each day and invite me to take my place. The sluice basin is unusable in the winter with the ground being frozen hard, yet it feels good to stand before it in the morning, with a little bowl of meltwater balanced in it, and meet my gaze in the mirror above it, watching myself wake up and come to life from under a cold, wet flannel. After a while, I can't imagine a nicer place than in front of the kitchen counter, with its tatty waxcloth covering. Here I make my breakfast, the aroma of coffee spreading from the pot on the cooker, and savour a cup by the window with its view across to the fjord. Halfway between the cold draught from the front door and the warmth of the stove, so contentedly absorbed in my own meditations that I jump every time a stack of burnt logs collapses and turns to ash.

Such moments could make me stay here for the rest of my life. A researcher on a never-ending field trip. I don't dwell on the things that aren't so positive, such as the lack of water here, the immense quantities of snow that have to be melted continually to deal with the dishes, the laundry and bodily fluids. Plates and cups tend to pile up, delicately glued together with dried crusts of cooking fat and gravy, while my dirty clothes, in particular the underpants that I put to soak in a bowl under the sluice basin, can stay there for days until the smell of stale water, detergent and dissolved secretions penetrates the already thick air. So far I have remained attentive to my daily ablutions, but I can occasionally see little signs that I live alone, away from other people's observant gaze and keen sense of smell. And then it occurs to me that I am like her, the woman who lived here before, that this was how she looked after months and years under virtually the same conditions. Hands and arms constantly flecked with soot, pale skin shiny with frying fat and sweat, hair in greasy streaks, combed and divided in a sharp parting, her body wrapped in a veil of smells from cooking and wood-burning, mixed with a distinct hint of the fragrances of unwashed cavities. I'm exaggerating, of course, on both our accounts, but I worry that this is how Jo sees me when we're on Skype: that, stripped of civilization's expectations of personal hygiene, it is the dregs of my decline that he sees unfold on his screen.

Truth be told, Jo has expressed a certain surprise during our last Skype conversations and has, if possible, seemed even more distant, especially after I got an infection in my wound and the skin across my cheek swelled up so much.

Or is it rising concern I sense, unease about my fall, the accident I had some weeks back? He might pass a hand over his nose, cup it around his mouth as though to prevent an outburst, and then in a hoarse voice exclaim: You're clearly getting stuck into your work.

Or: The conditions you're living under seem pretty brutal.

I laugh at him, mouth gaping, eyes like two black berries in narrow slits, and wonder if it really is me that I see in the corner of the screen.

39

I go out into the shed and head back with a basketful of fine, dry birch wood. Just outside the cabin I stop and stare across the landscape, my gaze fixed on a snow flurry that glitters like gold dust, a little cloud in the whirling wind, shot through with the sleepy afternoon light of the sun that peeps over the edge of the isthmus. I'm about to go in for my camera. I lean over to put down the basket, one hand on the door handle. But as I straighten up, I feel the unmistakable judder from my phone in my snowsuit pocket. A signal that tells me that I've received a text. It must be Jo, I say to myself out loud, feeling a quivering anticipation at what he may have written. I keep to plan and get the camera down from the hook, go out onto the steps and zoom in on the light phenomenon. I'll make myself a cup of coffee before I read his message. As if to demonstrate my willpower, I take more pictures than are strictly necessary. The snow flurry's playful gusts have ebbed away, but I continue to spin slowly around, zoom in, take snaps of the fjord, the peninsula and the shed. When I'm finally satisfied, I go inside and sit down at the plank table to load the images onto my PC, still wearing my outdoor gear with the phone in my pocket. I savour the knowledge of this unexpected communication, the deferred pleasure of reading each word, the fact that he, Jo, has something he wants to say to me outside the pre-arranged times. Our conversations are so halting and artificial precisely because we don't contact one another spontaneously, out of longing or desire, but because it is a duty, a forced and necessary responsibility.

It strikes me that fieldwork has many similarities to a stay on a space station. Like an astronaut I find myself in a desolate place, lonely and infinitely far from people, utterly dependent on technology as my sole link to the world beyond. A contact so structured, so focused on the functional, that any unexpected, personal enquiry feels like a loving embrace.

Half an hour has passed before I finally take off my scooter suit and put the satellite phone on the table, then it's another fifteen minutes before I sit down by the window with a cup of freshly brewed coffee to read the message. I've put some wood in the stove but haven't lit the wall lamps. The warmth and the sliver of light from the half-open vent have a calming effect, like the presence of a devoted animal. I take a sip of coffee, chew on a nail and, when my anticipation has built up to fever pitch, I see my fingers remove the phone from its protective cover, turn the display towards me, bring up the screen and open the inbox. I see too that the message is not from Jo but S. And that's all. With a click it's as though my gaze is locked fast, my fingers frozen in a tight grip.

Or is it the world around me that has stopped? When I turn to look towards the window, the sky seems lacerated by the sharp spikes of the fixed stars. The little glow that remains is draining away; my eyes tell me that by tomorrow the universe may be empty of light.

The stove goes out. An icy cold fills the room, creeps up through the floor and permeates the walls. I barely dare move or lift a finger for fear of triggering an avalanche.

I read the message over and over again until it looks like nothing but isolated words on a background of hard plastic and metal.

It might be read as follows: *Rumour you are Well more company.*

Or: *says not alone. Soon you*

Or simply as it is: *Rumour says you are not alone. Well, you'll have more company soon.*

Eventually I get up, my body stiff. And for the first time since my arrival here I turn the key in the lock. From now on this place will be divided into two. There is the cabin and the safety of the rooms within it. And then there is nature, the landscape, everything outside.

40

That spring, when you were thirty-two and I was thirty-one, two years before Lina was born, I stood and waited for you outside a cafe where a few of our friends were gathered. The asphalt was black and wet, the sky grey and overcast, it had rained all day. I was looking forward to celebrating your new job, after the final interview in a string of interviews before your eventual appointment. It's just a formality, you had said that morning. I stood in the nearby car park waiting for you, two hours after you were meant to have finished, one and a half hours after you were meant to arrive at the cafe, an hour after I had called you, and half an hour after your text telling me to meet you here and reserve a parking space. I was wearing a dress with straps, pale blue, and round my neck, on my chest, the silver heart you had given me for Christmas. I was freezing cold and needed a pee after too many beers, but I held on, kicking at the wet gravel with the tips of my thin shoes, until I felt the rainwater seeping between my toes, the dampness in the air clinging to my skin and hair, anxious for you not to see my realization that it had all gone wrong. I thought it best to act normally, for your pride. To give you the time you needed, before you might tell me yourself, with a passing comment, like: No, it didn't go as expected, but fuck it, there'll be other opportunities. I straightened up when I saw you drive towards me, casually smiled and waved as you parked the car. Through the window I saw you put on the handbrake, take the key out of the ignition in your usual self-assured way. But then, as you contemplated your next move, the coordination you'd need in your arms and legs to exit the car, I saw you hesitate. Instead of making a grab for the door handle and getting straight out, you sat there with clenched fists, staring out at me through the glass.

I find it hard to believe you'd been crying, but your eyes were sore, your eyelids red and swollen, and your gaze seemed to suck me in, so strange and direct. I opened the door for you, still keen to keep up the pretence, but in one swift move you got out of the car and pulled me to you. With your nose, your face in my hair, you sighed so violently, with such vulnerability, that without reservation or hesitation I whispered that I loved you.

Just six months later you had some friends round to your apartment to celebrate getting a job that offered the prospects you wanted. Or was it just an ordinary party? Whichever was the case, we sat on stools and boxes around the coffee table and the kitchen island, joined for the occasion into one long, split-level dining table. Later in the evening, in the glow of candles, hazy from generous quantities of wine and beer, we raised our glasses to you, several times. Glasses and bottles were clinked, followed by laughter and loud toasts to your friendship, but also your determination and great competitive spirit. All evening your gaze was fixed on me, unwaveringly, until suddenly, with an inscrutable smile, you got up and raised a hand to quieten the laughter and chatter. People exchanged glances, looked up at you expectantly, you grabbed a bottle from the table and fiddled with the neck, and I was sure you wanted to tell a joke. I smiled expectantly with the rest; it took several seconds before I realized what you were actually saying, that you were standing up to rattle off a tribute, a declaration of love to me.

You said that this job, your happiness and success were all thanks to me, your girlfriend. It was I who helped you to carry on, to give that little bit extra, not just because we were good together and I made you happy, but because... And here you stopped, put down the bottle and stroked your chin, emphasizing your uncertainty. Then, almost whispering, you said that I, who always seemed so strong and independent, often found things difficult and now that we knew each other better you realized that I was like most women, or at least that I wasn't as tough as people might think. You coughed, cleared your throat. Everyone looked at me. And then you went on to say that all you wanted was to see me happy and to give me the security, the love, that you knew I needed and sought. All you wanted was that I reciprocate one day, in the form of a home and family.

During this speech everyone's gaze flitted between you and me, and by the time you were done, a few eyes shone wet. Afterwards, in the toilet, my eyes were glinting too, but with anger, with an intense rage that made me want to scream and lash out. And because I couldn't see then, didn't understand what I've understood since, I interpreted my own rage as a sign of instability, a fundamental shortcoming that made me ask meaningless questions and turn everything good on end. Only years later, after the many unpleasant incidents and my demand for divorce, did I confront you with what those words had expressed so precisely. You're pathetic, I said. You want to limit me, to keep me trapped, helpless and weak, when you're the one who's helpless and weak, you miserable shit. You are small and scared and totally dependent on me.

41

16 February, nine o'clock in the evening. The Milky Way glitters over the bay and fjord, a backdrop against which the Northern Lights twist and turn across the sky like an acid-green snake. I am on my way out to the toilet but stop and stare at the electromagnetic dance that grows steadily more frenetic, the transformation of thin ribbons into a swathe of folds that quiver above me like the finest silk. The wind blows gently on the wind gauge, it is remarkably quiet and all that can be heard is the sea – the lap of waves and the rattle of pebbles.

As I stand staring up at the vault of the sky, I think of all the old superstitions and myths in which the Northern Lights are a vengeful entity that brings tragedy and destruction. If I wave a white kerchief it will come down and get me. So says the ancient myth. I picture myself as a child, my terror when this strange light play seemed drawn to the square of cloth I held between my fingers. Twenty-eight years later I should be brave enough to wave every sheet, towel or rag I possess, but with the situation as it is out here I don't even dare challenge an old wives' tale.

I'm coming to get you. That is the refrain of the Northern Lights, but also of this place here. It sings in the wind, behind the door of the privy, in the dark of the shed. I hear it whispered behind my footsteps, hummed outside the window as I lie down to sleep. I'm coming now. You will be held to account for what you have done, for what you have allowed to be lost through your carelessness. Yes, we have probably both experienced it, Borghild and I, the blame, the raging despair, manifest in our husbands' eyes, wild to the point of madness. We have felt the anxiety tingling in our fingers and toes, spreading through our bodies, overwhelming us with an all-pervasive nausea. And what I fear, she probably feared too, the moment of escalation, when the refrain changes from a distant threat to a shattering scream: Now you'll really get it!

Olaf no longer trusts her, that much has become clear with the passing months. His distrust is evident no matter what she does, making her feel deeply uncomfortable, yes, awkward, even with the children. He pursues her, watches her. His gaze is like the relentless draught from the cracks in the log walls, a constant chill across her shoulders and arms, even close to the stove, in the warmest part of the house. He appears from nowhere, out in the bay, in the shed or in the loft, as when earlier that summer, bent over the washtub and board, she suddenly felt him standing there, breathing down her neck. He can burst in rudely and order her to finish her work, as happened the day before last when she was frying potato pancakes over the stove. He never allows her a minute's peace, a moment's calm; a manifestation perhaps of his own inner state, an unremitting chase to and fro between his grief for Niels and rage at her irresponsibility. Or is his state caused by something entirely different, something she can't grasp or understand? His face. She dreams about it. It can come at her from any direction, distressed and distorted. Eventually she thinks she recognizes these dream-induced features in him when she's awake too. Then she realizes that her feelings for Olaf have been eroded, damaged to the core, leaving only a kernel of what was once love.

But there are no blows. No direct attacks. Only this one thing, a sense that something might happen, at any time, in any place and in any way. And perhaps the worst thing of all is this – the cord that tightens and releases, then tightens and releases again, the unease, the fear, the foreboding, after an event like this one at the bird cliff.

Kittiwakes' eggs are nutritious, but also highly valued goods that can be traded for cod liver oil, sugar and flour. For years she and Olaf have combined their efforts to collect them. The eggs that lie on the more accessible ledges, under the crevices that cut into the mountains, can be brought up quite simply with the help of 'egg spoons' on long poles. But when there are few eggs in sight, there is nothing for it but to climb down the cliff. And as she is little and light that task is always hers.

It was one of the first spring days after the fire. They walked from home in silence, Olaf some steps ahead of her. When they finally reached the cliff edge, their silence was still unbroken.

With a rope lashed about her waist and a basket over her shoulder, she started out on the steepest, firmest rock face, climbed down step by step, ledge by ledge, and in some places where there was no foothold she let herself be lowered, but never more than five or ten centimetres at a time. She had always had complete confidence in him and it was this, not the rope, that was the strongest bond between them at such moments. When she saw him disappear behind the edge and stood face to face with the rock, she felt safe. Confident in his strength, confident in his love, confident that all he wanted was to see her come back up safely.

All around her the kittiwakes flew to and from their nests; a few flapped very near, so close that she could feel the beat of their wings sweep over her back and hair. Furious, the birds tried to peck at her, but she drove them away as she snatched up their eggs. The ledges were smooth and slippery, covered with bird droppings, damp grass and moss, and in a split second of inattention she slipped and lost her balance. She grabbed at the rope, clung to it tightly, looked up and met his gaze high above her. He was holding her firmly, decisively, his arms steady, the rope strong, but like an avalanche she suddenly saw it: their bond was broken. In that instant she saw him let go of the rope, saw herself fall and rush towards the abyss, backwards, her skirts and apron billowing like a sail round her legs, saw herself disappear, grow smaller and smaller, until she was swallowed by the crashing sea far below.

It was in him that this took place, but she saw it all, what he wanted to do there and then. And she carries that picture with her like a disease that slowly drains her of strength.

42

Can I call it a form of self-treachery, this thing I am experiencing increasingly often? I not only dream in a woken state and detect unidentifiable sounds about me, but even solid objects, the most tangible things, seem to play little tricks on me. For example, I might put the knife down on the kitchen counter and find it later on the windowsill in the sleeping alcove. I'll put it back, very consciously, on the breadboard, but when I go to bed it's there on the windowsill again. The almanac vanished into thin air weeks ago, until I open a drawer one day and find it turned to 22 February. That might not be so strange in itself, but when it happens twice, I feel I am losing my grip.

I make a decision to sharpen up, to fine-tune my perception and to be more exacting in my contact with reality. The first and most obvious thing I can do is to establish a reliable relationship to the day's routines: that is, to carry out all my tasks at fixed times. From now on I intend to get up at exactly half past seven, eat breakfast at eight fifteen and, weather permitting, drive out to the bird cliff at eleven fifteen on the dot. I also plan to draw up a list of all my tasks and then make a timetable. These include:

fetching in wood, putting petrol in the scooter and generator, melting snow for washing the dishes and for my ablutions and, when required, cleaning, tidying and clearing snow. A pedantic and seemingly neurotic project to an outsider, but for a hermit an exact breakdown of activities is the only way to punctuate the days. The recording of weather, temperature, wind speed, humidity, air pressure and precipitation will of course continue as before, and these parameters, coupled with my new routines, will, I assume, give me the necessary sense of perspective and control.

But there is still something I can't grasp. A kind of disturbance at the bottom of everything. Something of magnitude that I cannot explain, name or adequately describe. Whenever I try, I think of it as a hazy sketch of snowdrifts and ice in faint, almost erased lines. Like when I stood at the cooker one day heating a can of food and light suddenly flooded in through the window, crossing the floor before disappearing. When I looked outside, a thick layer of cloud decked the isthmus like a cloak, but further south there was a gash in the cloud cover, revealing a bottomless sky that swept across the bay with an astounding blue-green light. It was as though a miracle were happening, right there, outside the cabin. If I try to hold the thought, the image literally dissolves, scrawled lines crossing every which way that flare up then disappear, a flash of stars against a background that rumbles and quakes, sudden smoke, endless expanses. But these are merely words, a banal packaging of sensations I cannot place. Like the gentle tug on my shirtsleeve as I sit absorbed in my work, or the light stroke of my hair as I drift off to sleep, or the feeling of being held back when I'm about to go out of the door. The impression is of breath and life and existence. Or perhaps it is just my unconscious longing for human contact.

But this indefinable something expresses itself in other ways too. It's about ten past eleven in the morning. I have filled the tank on the scooter, and gone in and out of the cabin to fetch the equipment I need for my trip to the bird cliff. Finally I'm ready. The front door is shut, my satellite phone is in my inside jacket pocket and my PC is in the storage box under the seat of the scooter, along with the emergency beacon, some drinks and provisions. Small tasks, small actions that I've carried out so often I barely need to think about what I'm doing. I put on my gloves and adjust my balaclava and goggles, before settling onto the seat with my hands on the steering bar. It's possible that I sit idly for a second, that I examine the sky, let my gaze follow what's left of the tracks from my previous day's trip, but then as I squeeze my legs around the tank, lift my hand to press the start button, right then, in that action, I feel it. Something or other outside me gets aboard, squeezing itself down behind me. I feel a pressure on my back and along my thighs, a weight against my chest, as though I'm being held tightly, gripped by two strong arms, so hard that I have to gasp for breath.

This feeling, this indefinable something, always comes very quickly and then, before I can take it in or experience it consciously, it's gone. My nervous system responds to the event with goosebumps that can last for minutes. I have observed certain variations, nuances between what I register either inside or outside the cabin. Inside, these episodes seem coloured by my desire for attention, some kind of caring and tenderness, while outside the opposite seems true. Surrounded by the wind, the temperature, the air pressure, the parameters I measure and observe so painstakingly, I sense a threat, that it is here, the thing I should evade, the thing I fear.

Over and over again, I reprimand myself: Sharpen up! From now on you mustn't think of either S or those who once lived here.

43

But I have to think about something. Particularly in the evenings, which arrive much too early. By the afternoon my tasks are complete and my timetable is empty. A storm is raging again, and until it stops, I spend the last idle hours of the day in the rocking chair in front of the stove.

I think about Lina. She's always with me anyway, but even the best and brightest images just depress me.

I think about Jo, about our conversations, about his living room and his superb taste, his furniture, his things, the soundtrack on his music system, soft female voices and delicate guitar riffs. Again I undress him, unbutton his shirt, pull down his trousers, slide my hands over his stomach, through the wreath of hairs that go into a dark point from his navel, and think about his erection, taut and powerful, the faint odour of the salty sea. I picture the blood vessels on the underside of his cock, the traffic system from and to the heart, the blood transported in and the blood led back, red and blue, hot and cold, nearness and distance, and soon I am lost in thoughts of promises made and broken, hope followed by disappointment, his vacillation and indecision. As the pressure locks itself in my throat, hard and tight, I stop and divert my stream of thoughts somewhere else entirely.

I think of the scooter, its power, the sound of the motor and the fierce acceleration, and imagine myself in wide-open terrain, speeding wildly over the snowdrifts with a sweet tingling in my chest, then lifting off, and after flying slowly through the air, shoulders hunched, eyes focused straight ahead, I see myself land with the rifle over my shoulder and then I see the towering figure of S in the bow of the captain's boat. Again, I quickly turn my thoughts elsewhere, the bird cliff, my research, all the data, and for a moment I manage to focus on some serious issues, such as the worrying decline in nesting populations. Seabirds are at the top of the food chain and extra sensitive to pollution, climate change and shifts in the nutrient base. As many as sixteen out of twenty-eight species with habitats along the coast are now red-listed, categorized as 'near threatened', 'vulnerable', 'endangered' or 'critically endangered'. Which reminds me of the situation I find myself in here, utterly alone, in a vulnerable place and with the threat of a visit hanging over me. An intolerable idea, one that I can't handle. And now that I'm conscious of it, of how limited my world has become in this boundless landscape, I realize with horror that even my rational thoughts have been consigned to a remote corner of my brain.

With mild disinterest I register the storm's raging

gusts against the wall. I press my feet to the floor, push the rockers on my chair back and lift my toes. The air current produced by the rocking motion is liberatingly fresh.

44

19 February. Six weeks and four days after my arrival. The time is sixteen hours and thirty-one minutes. The temperature at the kitchen counter is twenty degrees. Near the rocking chair, approximately one and a half metres from the stove, the temperature is twenty-five degrees Celsius, while the slushy, half-melted snow in the bucket by the sluice basin has a temperature of one point three degrees. The temperature outside is minus two point four. The wind comes from the west at a rate of nine point six metres per second. Cloud cover is six eighths. The sun, less than six degrees below the horizon, emits a brightness of four hundred lux or thereabouts. It is now sixteen hours and thirty-three minutes and I can hear the following sounds: a crackling from the stove, a slight howl from the wind that squeezes through the crack between the front door and the door frame, mixed with the steady drone of the generator, not dissimilar to the sound of an electric lawn-mower, which according to the manufacturer's brochure has a noise level of approximately sixty-five decibels. I pour my fourth cup of coffee. The inside of my mouth is rough and dry, although this is a subjective observation,

as opposed to my pulse, which is 110, and my respiratory rate, which is twenty-four breaths per minute. Clinically speaking, my skin is clammy and cold. I assume that my blood pressure has increased significantly and my pupils are enlarged. An acute nausea churns in my solar plexus, a churning sea of mackerel in tomato sauce that I try to both shift and hold back. I walk around the cabin, dizzy and faint, conscious of only one thing: that part of me that wants to disappear, transcend, turn into air, nothingness. A wish that my body, with the help of my sympathetic nervous system, instantly and mercilessly fulfils by opening all channels. I rush out to the toilet and empty myself with a loud moan. After writhing for a full five minutes over the polystyrene toilet seat, my face as much as my arse over the pool of muck, I am completely exhausted. My legs and arms are trembling from both the cold and the physical strain. At the same time I feel almost relieved, ready, and while I clean myself with the wet wipes, I try to recall the moment that triggered this reaction.

As part of my new structured routine, I have set myself the task of transferring the data from the bird cliff to a new document. I also intended to sort out my photographs to make it easier for me to observe the gradual change in snow conditions in the terrain. But before I could put the data into bar charts, I needed to enter the figures that had been collected on a spreadsheet. And that was when things broke down. Or rather, that was when I discovered my unbelievable error. All my data collections were suddenly logged under the year 1871. When a jam-packed hard disk is put under stress the date settings are easily messed up. And something similar can doubtless happen to a data logger. Snow and ice are known to affect both signals and measurements on occasion. But why 1871? A completely anachronistic mistake. And that wasn't all. When I compared my notes with the logged data, I found unacceptable discrepancies. For example, at eleven o'clock on 14 February I noted a fresh breeze from the north of ten point three metres per second and a temperature of minus one point two degrees Celsius. By contrast, the data logger gave a temperature of minus thirteen point six and a moderate breeze from the south-west of six metres per second. Indeed, the logged data indicated lower temperatures throughout and there was no record of any wind as strong as the one I had experienced some days back. It was then, in a moment, entirely subsumed by my imagination and with bits of mackerel grinding about in my belly, that I began to believe that the data was actually from 1871, or to be precise from the winter weeks preceding the unspecified tragedy, one year after the fire. And once this fantasy was kindled and cast its red-hot glow over everything, I started to think that even my photographs confirmed this conclusion. After all, weren't the quantities of snow in the pictures far larger than any I had observed up until now with my own sharp eyes? And the shed, didn't it appear newly built in the snapshots I'd taken during the light phenomenon over the plain?

A sensory disturbance caused by acute food poisoning is the most obvious explanation, I tell myself, as I close the door to the outside toilet. But when I sit at my table and check the data series again, the same figures shine out at me, the same unrecognizable records set in a completely different century. And yes, the same goes for the pictures. The quantities of snow do indeed seem bigger, the shed newer, like some sort of forceful reminder that the science of meteorology is built on chaos.

I pace about the cabin restlessly, in some useless attempt to remove myself, but when I look in the window it is my own reflection I see, and when I go into the kitchen it is my gaze I meet in the mirror. I walk on into the sleeping alcove, where it is my body that has left its impression in the mattress, and it is the movements of my legs and arms that have caused crumples in the sheet and duvet. The dust between the legs of the bed comes from me, from my bedding and clothes, mixed perhaps with hair from my pubic area and head, and a microscopic sprinkling of scurf from the very outer layer of my skin. On the kitchen counter, it is my mess that is piling up, my debris, my leftovers, and when I close my eyes it is my odour I smell, a mix of my sweat, my intestinal gases, my breath, my metabolism, my own unstoppable, clammy presence. And when I cast another glance over the data, all the observation notes and statistics, I see nothing but my own theories, my own apocalyptic fantasies.

45

After all these irrational events, passing impressions, disembodied sounds, the time has come to confront myself, to ask the cause, directly and ruthlessly. Although one explanation will ultimately be as ambiguous as another. I might of course have driven myself to insanity, brought on by pure loneliness and displaced emotions. I might also have been deeply disturbed by my feelings of guilt about leaving Lina, by my longing for her and Jo, and my frustration at Jo's hesitation and doubt. My fears for the seabird populations may have had an effect too. I see threats everywhere. It is also possible that everything can be attributed to my relationship with S, to the constant underlying fear of his impulsive actions and manipulative games. The least feasible cause is the one I hardly dare contemplate. This *something* – this sinister *something* in this place. Is it real, concrete? Am I feeling an intangible presence that any other person in my position would have felt? A presence that no one could identify or explain rationally? So far I have no answer. I think of everything human beings are unable to perceive, such as the earth's magnetic field, by which some birds, fish and insects can navigate.

The question appears to be: What am I not seeing?

It's coming up to six, the time when Jo and I meet on Skype. Four days after our last screen meeting and two days after our last phone call. It feels like an eternity. Time goes infinitely slowly in my spaceship, day and night float together, and the abiding void inside as well as outside attests to the standstill. I should feel free here, away from the world as I am, but I have never felt more closed in.

I go to the kitchen counter, the area in the cabin where I can usually Skype without too much interference, and here I connect my PC to the satellite phone, open the screen and switch it on. The light comes on gradually like a sunrise, before radiating a powerful blue-white into the darkened room. Like the light from an ambulance, or a floodlight in the city. If only I could crawl into that light and feel that I was safe for a moment; that the challenges I am facing now were merely transient, like a superficial infection. Not unlike the feeling I often get with Jo, a feeling that now, now everything will be better.

Like on our first trip, a hike on a clear autumn day to a mountain peak just above the city. We walked along cliff edges, zigzagged up gentle inclines and clambered up steep slopes, breathing and sweating at an even tempo, until two and a half hours later we stood at the top. We hugged each other, said nothing, absorbed in the dizzying view, sea and islands and mountains, the sight of the horizon, the gossamer mist over the mouth of the fjord, the drama of the rock formations in the far distance. Then we walked over to a rock covered in deep green lichen to eat our packed lunch sheltered from the wind. The mountain was covered by a thin layer of moss and when I went to sit down Jo held me back, said wait, folded my groundsheet double and lay his scarf on it. I liked it so much, this show of consideration, and as we sat there with the thermos between us, eating our sandwiches, I asked him straight out what he thought of me. It surprised him that I could ask him such a direct question – I could see that from the way he threw the last morsel into his mouth and thoughtfully chewed. But when he turned to me, it was with a warm and open gaze, and with his head close to mine he said that I was amazingly tough and tenacious, that was the best he could say, at least now, on this trip. We sipped our coffee and laughed, and even if his answer wasn't quite what I'd hoped for, I appreciated his description of me, as these were precisely the qualities I was going to need. Tough and tenacious to tackle S and his aggression, tough and tenacious to get through the hurt that awaited me, tough and tenacious in my conviction that things would turn out well in the end.

Freedom. I saw it in the view, in the outstretched horizon, but it was also there between us, and it flew forth and launched itself like an eagle from the sheerest cliff.

But it has crashed, this freedom. It lies here in the cabin, brought to the ground by unforeseen phenomena and events. I stand here in front of my PC, more shaky and exhausted than tough and tenacious. I call Jo, and there it is again, his face, more wonderful than I remember,

warmer and safer than ever. I stretch out a finger and stroke
the screen, tease what's expected out of myself: first some
questions about how things are at home, then a bit about
the weather here. I'm holding it together by a thread, I can
hear it in my voice as it cracks and skids on the vowels.
While I chatter on, his eyes narrow and a frown appears
between his brows. I hear him interrupt, ask if something
has happened, but I go on at length about trivialities – yesterday's petrol consumption and the litres of snow that
I've melted. How can I tell him about all the things that I
am sensing and feeling, when I hardly dare acknowledge
them to myself? I don't want to say them aloud, to confirm
for my surroundings, for the things in the cabin, for this
something, that it has been registered, taken in. Because
then it will no longer be fantasy, a mere sense of unease,
but fixed and concrete, and inescapably present.

Jo leans forward. He is clearly scrutinizing my image
on the screen, which I find reassuring. He is listening to
me, seeing me. I say the only possible thing, the only thing
I can and want to say:

I say: You must come now.

I say: Come now.

I say: Come.

And as I say this, chant it out loud, I see myself in the
corner of the screen, the way my fingers tug at my top
round my hips, pull the wool garment up out of my trousers and further over my stomach, up to my neck, I see my
breasts, their curves dictated by their weight, the nipples,
red and hardened from the draught, and I see my hands

slide round my midriff, move to these two body parts, lift them up and hold them forward until the soft, white flesh fills the entire picture. And then, just as I nearly fall over the screen, I hear Jo's voice, subdued and gentle:

Jo says: My darling one.

Jo says: I realize that you need me.

Jo says: It's serious now.

46

The diversity (within the parameters of my research and interest):

Kittiwake; Northern Fulmar; Common Gull; Great Black-backed Gull; Great Cormorant; European Shag; Parasitic Jaeger; Common Murre; Thick-billed Murre; Black Guillemot; Razor-billed Auk; Atlantic Puffin; Common Eider; King Eider; the Captain; Gry; Maria; S; Jo; Lina

Red-listed (within the same research and interest area):

Kittiwake; Northern Fulmar; Common Gull; Parasitic Jaeger; Common Murre; Thick-billed Murre; Black Guillemot; Razor-billed Auk; Atlantic Puffin; Common Eider; Me

47

20 February. There's a huge weather shift on its way, caused by yet another storm that has wreaked havoc all night. I heard the rain lashing against the windows for hours, while my hands gripped the bed frame, ready to cling on if the cabin was swept into the sea in a gust of wind. How many storms can these walls withstand before they loosen and yield to the pressure? The storm eventually quietens down over the course of the morning; when I get up, all that can be heard is the wind tinkering with the roof felt. I get dressed, pour water into the kettle and light the gas, and while the water is heating I walk over to the front door and open it. A rush of air sweeps into the room, surprisingly pleasant and mild, but as I stand in the doorway and stare at what I can make out of land and sea in a hazy morning light, all that's visible is devastation. The ravages inflicted by the storm on the shed's panelled walls are one thing, but what really makes an impression is the volume of snow that has been scrubbed away in this harsh attack. Huge areas of the landscape have been laid bare: rocks and blades of withered grass protrude here and there, like wounds, a rash only partially hidden by a bandage.

All I want is to normalize the situation. And the most normal thing I can do now is to drive out to the bird cliff and replace the data logger in an attempt to rectify the error I discovered yesterday. Wearing nothing but my woollens, I venture out in front of the cabin to assess the conditions further, but after just a few hesitant steps I can see it will be impossible to drive all the way out there. The change of weather has turned the snow to slush. In exposed areas the slopes are already muddy over the frozen earth beneath, and here and there light glints on ice floes that have been hidden in deep snow.

This certainly isn't down to S at least, I think, as I consider putting on my snowshoes. I ought not to leave it untried, it must be possible to get there on foot. I can set out now with my rucksack and, if my assessment of the conditions is correct, I should be at the bird cliff by about twelve thirty. But then I stop myself. Deviations from the normal, from what should be fieldwork in relatively safe circumstances, are too frequent and overwhelming now.

As I wander about, I ask myself what makes me want to take on these obstacles. How many storms can I withstand before the walls within me loosen and yield to the pressure? I toil with these questions as much as with the slushy snow, and when I slip and feel the water seeping into my woollen garments, I resolve to get an answer, a proper and substantial answer. I shall do so while I clean myself up.

48

I stand naked with my feet in a bowl in the middle of the cabin. A kettle stands on a stool beside me and in a calm, repeated motion I pour lukewarm melted snow from it over my head, neck and chest. In the light of the wall lamps, beneath the water's glinting surface, the dirt streams away. A stripe is visible in the fold around my stomach, grime has collected between my breasts and round my armpits, and when I pass the cloth over my neck and down to my chest, it darkens with soot and old sweat. The water trickles and splashes and drips, little puddles collect on the black plastic sheet around the bowl. I wash and scrub myself just as the storm did in its brutal attack, and soon my skin is like the landscape outside, scoured bare with rocks and stones and patches of wild grass.

As I wash myself, I am determined that something, just something, will emerge and become clear. That by scrubbing and rubbing I will penetrate the layers of dirt and grime until I can see myself with absolute clarity. I wash and rinse my hair, lather myself with soap and lose myself in my body, its very presence, my stomach, breasts, thighs, those parts of me which belonged to Lina, but which have also been desired by S and Jo, and suddenly I am standing in the bowl like a carved-up object of prey, owned and marked by all three. Despite my desire for self-governance I am aware that I possess territories that do not obey me, and do the opposite of what I need or want.

In this situation, for example:

There's a ring at the door of my new apartment. S is standing outside. He smiles and says that he's come to pick up Lina's woollen jumper, which she left behind after her stay with me that weekend. I'm a little surprised at the timing of his visit. Lina has just been dropped off at the kindergarten and the weather's pretty mild, but I want to be cooperative so I ask him to wait while I go in and get it. He smiles again, pushes the door open and steps inside, saying how nice it would be to see where Lina lives when she's with me. Still determined to show willingness, but also careful not to trigger his anger, I let him in, and ask him to wait in the hallway while I go to the bathroom and fetch the jumper out of the laundry basket. He comes after me, of course. All the way to the washing machine. I hand him the jumper, which he doesn't take but throws indifferently back into the basket. It needs washing, he says. My gaze instinctively follows the little garment and then, as I look back at him, dubious, a little annoyed, he answers by grabbing my arm and pressing me up against the wall.

I can see from his expression what I should do now. I should put up some resistance, lash out with my arms and legs, and if that fails, I should stop him with my fingers, tug, pinch, claw, but I can see how angry he'll get, how much more aroused, and I can see that he's already there, in that place where he can lose himself, become violent, perhaps dangerous. And here, right here, I am near the answer, the core of myself. The weak spot that S so self-assuredly pointed out. This is where the walls within me crumble. If I am scared enough, I give in.

Like one of those birds that play dead, I sink to the floor, bend to his body, make myself available even, close my eyes and move with him. As though something in me wants to, because it was good once. As if there's something in me that has to, because I'm just a cunt. That's how he regards me, as I lie there. But what he doesn't know, cannot understand, is that I've already disappeared. I'm not there on the bathroom floor under his body, but somewhere far away, beyond him, in a place that is totally removed from what's happening, where he can never, never reach me.

49

22 February, eleven o'clock. Observation near the cabin. Temperature: six point two degrees Celsius. Wind: a light breeze from the north-west, two point one metres per second. Cloud cover: eight eighths. Nimbostratus.

Water drips from the roof and down the walls, trickles from the heaps of old snow and collapsed snow dunes, forming tiny rivulets that gather into a stream that rushes past my front door and down to the shore. The fog hangs white and thick over the bay, and from where I am, outside the door, it seems to be expanding and slowly rolling closer. I'm not sure if I should see this phenomenon as beguiling or another wall that limits my existence. When the shed and scooter can't be seen, are they enveloped or have they vanished from the world? I can feel everything pressing in from all around. I go back inside, close the door and settle in the chair before the stove.

I sit there gazing into the glow from the open vent, lost in thoughts of shifting temperatures, warmth and cold, heat and ice, until an image pops into my mind from the bird cliff, of myself as a sensitive, wandering measuring instrument. I don't know whether it's this standstill, the fact that I'm prevented from driving out to the weather station to do my job, but this thought, this image, refuses to leave me. On the contrary, I see it increasingly clearly, my head, my arms, my legs, my hands and feet like tentacles, sucking in sensations and impressions, disquietude and intangible hidden states, without end. At the same time, probably as a result of the errors in my data, the gap between the dates and observations, I see that my figures and statistics are crumbling and crashing down, and that I, cornered in the world by absolute laws and regulations, made concrete and defined in units and values, that I, a human being, am falling through a gap between two measurements, in the distance between A and B, the void between one and two, the gap between numbers of degrees, hectopascals and metres per second. I fall and I find myself in an unclassifiable space, diffused, filled with riddles and uncertainty, but also with intense sensations, and in reaction to this image I rock my chair faster, back and forth, oscillating from one extreme point to the other, between then and now.

And there I see her, Borghild. She is sitting, as I am, abandoned to her thoughts. About Olaf, the change in him, their life out here. It can't go on. The house, this little place of theirs, yes, sorrow itself. She must tell him what she is thinking and she must do it now.

Borghild gets up, grabs her apron and skirts between her hands and goes out to the shed. She opens the door, shouts his name needlessly loudly – she realizes that from the silence that answers her from the walls. The sheep shift restlessly. She leans against the beams of their stall and their animal eyes stare back at her, their gaze fixed while their jaws continue uninterruptedly to chew on some straggly bits of straw. What are they trying to say? she wonders, her gaze probing the darkened corners of the shed. But no, not even a child could hide in there. She gathers her skirts again and walks towards the shoreline, where she stops, stares out with a hand up to her eyes. Is he out there on the fjord, casting his nets? She runs to the boathouse, pulls the sliding door aside. The boat is inside, brought up from the water. When she calls out to him again without answer, his absence is disturbingly palpable. She runs her fingers over the gunwale, around the oarlocks, as she would once have stroked him. Back outside, in the pale daylight, she jumps when the ice between two large pebbles cracks apart under the sole of her shoe. This feeling of high alert, she hates it, and pulls her shawl over her shoulders more tightly. Where can he have gone? The sea beyond the fjord is endlessly wide, the bay and isthmus are long and surrounded by crags. If he's not here, he can't have gone far; he hasn't got any food with him and he'll soon get cold in his old wadmal jacket. She sinks to her knees in loose snow, tramping over snowdrifts. When she shouts, it comes suddenly, and she stretches the words out, syllable by syllable, yelling as loudly and clearly as she can and until her voice is indistinguishable from an animal's scream in this desolate, empty space. I am leaving you! she yells with clenched fists. I am taking the girls and going back to town! She hears it herself, the disquiet she triggers. Or is it the opposite? Is the disquiet already around her? Is it disapproval, disgust and loathing she feels in the wind and in the darkness beneath the crags? She shudders. Thinks it, feels it, that Olaf is here, nearby. Unwilling to make himself known. Soon she goes home, closing the door firmly behind her.

50

I must have fallen asleep in the chair. It is already half past four and the cabin is pitch-dark. I stretch, switch on the wall lamps and go out to the privy, but on my way back I stop at the front door, struck again by the warmth in the air. I check the thermometer: the temperature has risen to plus nine point five degrees Celsius, despite the sun having set well below the horizon. I turn, stare at the steaming, fog-darkened wall. Here is the proof, I think. Of the collapse. The man-made madness. Concerned, but with my senses turned outwards, towards the weather phenomenon that's taking place right here outside the cabin, I become aware of an unfamiliar noise. All around me, from all directions, there is a streaming cacophony of gurgling and dripping and trickling. But amidst this din, these burbling sounds, I hear a rhythmic crunching or cracking sound that grows in strength as I stand here. I feel a pressure on my chest, breathe shallowly, focus on my senses, listen for the source of a sound, what it resembles, reminds me of, how it can be explained within the given conditions of the environment. It is far from unfamiliar. On the contrary, it's a sound I hear every day as I walk across the bay or along the seashore, but then it is steady and unvarying in its strength and rhythm, because it comes from me. Footsteps. I am hearing footsteps, and having separated their velocity and weight from the animal kingdom, I know that it is no stray reindeer or moose I can hear wandering out there. It is an adult human being, coming this way. I stand motionless, taking this in, before I clench my fists, hunch over, fill my chest, stretch up and yell: Jo! Jo! Is it you? I'm here! I bring my hand to my mouth, bite my knuckles, and at that moment I hear the footsteps slow down and come to a halt somewhere in the darkness and fog. There isn't a sound to be heard. I call out again: Jo! I'm here! The silence that follows is like a long parenthesis, but suddenly the footsteps are there again, careful, cautious as they draw closer. Something is wrong. I hear it in the hesitation, in the rhythm of feet in the wet snow, expectant, on guard. I yell out again. And I am taken aback by how loudly I scream, but also by the fact that I articulate S's name in full, and with a force that crashes through the thumping heartbeat in my throat. Is that you? I yell. Is that you, S, you bastard?

I don't listen for an answer, but go inside and lock the door, decisively and emphatically.

Indoors, there's a blessed feeling of stability and normality: the plank table stands as firmly as before and the rocking chair is as I left it just minutes ago. I go to the mirror, pinch my cheek, examine the effect, my own gaze. I am a little pale perhaps, but alert and clear-headed. I turn, look around me, absorb the sight of the pan on the cooker, the bucket of meltwater, the calm, the security they exude, their practicality of form and predictability of use, the aspects which make these objects most real and concrete, because now I hear a knock on the door.

My first thought is to grab my satellite phone, turn it on, go round the room to get a connection and call for help. A glance out of the window tells me that this is futile, as futile as spending time on the phone at all, for who could come to my aid in just a few minutes? Instead, I go over to the kitchen counter, take out the box of cartridges, then lift the rifle down from the hook on the wall and load it. Tasks executed by my hands swiftly and confidently, but I seem to observe these movements from the outside, far removed from the drama that has so suddenly arisen. If it isn't S who's standing out there, it might well be the captain, I say to myself. Yes, it's probably him, he's just the sort to sneak up on someone. No, it's more likely to be Jo – Jo, who has realized the gravity of the situation and wants to surprise me. I take another look out of the window, as if the answer might be found there instead of behind the door. But as my gaze hits the misty, steamed-up pane, I ask myself the question I ought to have asked at the start: How could a person find their way in this pitch-darkness? Head for the cabin with such certainty, precision? Who or what is actually out there?

There's another knock. This time it's so hard that the door itself shudders. A dual perception, both vibration and sound. That proves I'm not filled with imaginary sensations, I think, as I position myself near the entrance, legs astride and focused.

In a single movement I turn the key and raise the rifle, place the butt against my shoulder and aim the barrel at the door. With my finger on the trigger, cold and steady, I draw my breath three times. I draw breath, think of Lina, of the birds' arrival and of the life that will continue, before I shout loudly and clearly: Come in!

2020

Peirene STEVNS TRANSLATION PRIZE

The Peirene Stevns Translation Prize was launched in 2018 to support up-and-coming translators.

Open to all translators without a published novel, this prize looks not only to award great translation but also to offer new ways of entry into the world of professional translation. The winner receives a £3,000 commission to translate a text selected by Peirene Press, the opportunity to spend two months at a retreat in the Pyrenees and a dedicated one-on-one mentorship throughout the translation process.

The Peirene Stevns Prize focuses on a different language each year and is open for submissions from October to January.

With thanks to Martha Stevns, without whom this prize would not be possible.

Subscribe

Discover the best of contemporary European literature: subscribe to Peirene Press and receive a world-class novella from us three times a year, direct to your door. The books are sent out six weeks before they are available in bookshops and online.

Your subscription will allow us to plan ahead with confidence and help us to continue to introduce English readers to the joy of new foreign literature for many years to come.

'A class act.' GUARDIAN

'Two-hour books to be devoured in a single sitting: literary cinema for those fatigued by film.'

TIMES LITERARY SUPPLEMENT

A one-year subscription costs £35 (3 books, free p&p for UK)

Please sign up via our online shop at www.peirenepress.com/shop

WOMEN FOR REFUGEE WOMEN

Peirene is proud to support
Women for Refugee Women.

Women for Refugee Women is a UK-based charity
that supports women who are seeking asylum
and challenges the injustices they experience. The
charity runs a range of activities for refugee women,
including English classes, drama and writing
workshops, with the aim of empowering them to
tell their own stories. Women for Refugee Women
also advocates for a fairer asylum process and
works towards a world in which all women who
cross borders have the right to liberty, safety
and dignity.

www.refugeewomen.co.uk   CHARITY NUMBER 1165320